PIECE OF SHIT LOSER SCUMBAG

THIS IS NOT A MEMOIR

MATT MICHELI

ISBN: 979-8-218-92625-0

Prior Publication Acknowledgments
Fuck City Girls was most recently published by *Horror, Sleaze, Trash*. *Pretty Meat* was originally published by *Martian Lit*. *The Story of the Bear Man* was originally published by *Cease, Cows Magazine*. *The Day Seemed Endless* was originally published *by Slit Your Wrists Magazine*. *Love thy Neighbor* was published in *ABC's of Terror, vol. IV*. *Words* was originally published in *Red Fez Magazine*.

Cover art: Ira Rat
Formatting: Scarlett R. Algee

This collection is a culmination of stories written over the last eighteen-plus years. A lot has changed in that time. Back then, I was young and dumb and... (you know the rest) before settling down with the love of my life and becoming a husband and later a father. I've been writing off and on over that stretch, more off than on, but I somehow always find my way back. Because writing, like other forms of art, is a creative release, and humans—people—need that release to function properly in the rest of our lives. It helps us cope and compartmentalize things, express things. It helps us grieve. I came back to writing four years ago just as my family began our biggest fight ever, my wife's leukemia battle. And throughout this battle, when I found time even for an hour or so when I wasn't caring for my wife or taking care of my daughter, typing words was something I could hold onto. Something I could control. Because nothing else was able to be held or controlled. I was able to create stories, dictate the outcomes, determine what happened next. If only I had that power over real life.

This book and all others are dedicated to my wife—the love of my life—who now looks down on me and the kid from high above, which I am forever grateful for.

I love you always, honey.

Thank you to all the readers and fans who have reached out and shown support, bought books, shared reviews, messaged your thoughts and prayers. I am truly blessed and grateful. Much love, like...*all* of it.

CONTENTS

FUCK CITY GIRLS
9

THE APPLE
18

THE STORY OF THE BEAR MAN
30

PRETTY MEAT
34

THE COMPLEXITIES OF TIME AND WHAT NOT
40

THE LOOK
47

WORDS, MISERABLE FUCKING WORDS
53

LOVE THY NEIGHBOR
59

MY FIRST TIME WITH JESSIE SPANO: A FLASH PIECE
70

LOVE AND SADNESS AND FADING MEMORIES
73

AND THE DAY SEEMED ENDLESS
90

THE BOX
99

AUTHOR'S NOTE

ACKNOWLEDGMENTS

ABOUT THE AUTHOR

OTHER WORKS

PIECE
OF SHIT
LOSER
SCUMBAG

FUCK CITY GIRLS

I remember that summer like it was yesterday or even today. It was smoldering hot, hotter than it had been in years, hot enough to get into the record books and have the weathermen toss the terms "hottest day" and "record highs" around loosely and frequently. That was the summer I graduated high school and made up my mind that attending college at least a city away from here was best. I broke it off with my high-school sweetheart. She cried. I didn't. I packed up. My parents, looking at my one suitcase and duffel bag, asked if I was leaving for the semester or just a weekend. I said my goodbyes and was on my way. I was leaving it all behind, everything, everyone, the only world I had ever known, to venture into the exciting unknown.

I got settled into my dorm that looked more like a large bare-walled closet with beds, unpacking what little I brought with me. I met my new roommate, who seemed weird—he had a soft and sweaty handshake—who just left his boxes on his bed unopened. Later that night, the boxes were still there. The next morning, they remained untouched. I wondered if I'd ever see him again.

This new world known as college-in-the-city was definitely different from what I was used to. Back home was a small town of only several thousand where the Dairy Queen was the coolest spot to hang out after school and the local grocery store was the primary place of employment. The people in the city... It was somewhat refreshing to meet people that weren't cheerleaders or football players, and who weren't blonde-haired and blue-eyed. The party scene was unbelievable with more booze, drugs, techno, and young women throwing their inner selves at you (that's putting it lightly) than I could've ever imagined—bass thumping, girls dancing, everyone high on something. These were *real* parties, not like the little high school get-togethers involving a keg and a few bottles of Boone's Farm.

I remember meeting her. She was cute, and so were her friends. Their clothes were straight out of the punk scene from the 80's—torn fishnet stockings, lots of lime green and fluorescents, combat boots—ugly, but hip. Sexy. She was so free-spirited. They all were, laughing and smoking and dancing around in public, not giving a fuck about what anyone thought of them. And her eyes... She didn't look at you. She looked *in* you. I had never met anyone like her. All the girls back home came from the same Republican-conservative-cheerleader factory. They were all beautiful, but in that small-town look-like-all-their-friends sort of way, like they were molded from perfection—blonde, toned, perfect teeth, clean clothes. Not her. Not by a long shot. She was different and as far from the perfect I knew as you could get. And this difference drew me in like a fucking magnet.

Before I knew it, I was smitten over her, and she appeared to be smitten over me. And the sex... it was wetter and wilder than any world I had been to. Sex with her felt like freedom. Or maybe that was just the drugs that made it seem that way.

She and I had been hanging out for a couple weeks, and that day, we went to the mall. I remember how hot it was, and how I couldn't remember a day ever feeling this hot back home. We goofed around. She was so playful. She hit me and slapped my ass, and I slapped hers. She grabbed my crotch in front of everyone, which was kind of embarrassing but also exciting. We laughed and laughed about anything and anyone unfortunate enough to cross our field of vision: fat people, Asians, want-to-be punkers, the old guy with giant calves and tall socks. I remember her flicking her lit cigarette on the ground after being told that there was no smoking allowed. That was right after she took a long, slow puff, staring dead-on at the security guard, and blew smoke right in his face. I was stunned. That was probably the most rebellious and coolest thing I had ever seen. The look on the guard's face was priceless: angry but too shocked to react, a look of total disbelief, or maybe disgust.

Later on, we walked past one of those sunglass places, and there were these big fluorescent green Wayfarers. She grabbed them and put them on and posed in the mirror and posed some more—turned this way and that way. By that point, she had drawn a couple other admiring fans.

"Those are awesome," I said to her.

"I want them," she said.

I bought them for her, despite never spending that much money on anyone or myself ever before.

After that, we had some ice cream in the food court and then went and met some of her friends at an outdoor downtown café. It was in the heat of the day, and it must have been one-hundred degrees out there, but no one except me seemed to care that our own sweat was dripping into our drinks and our food. We sat around in this God-awful heat, sweating profusely, while they discussed bands I'd never heard of and she showed off her new expensive shades. Her friends loved them. I felt good about buying them but wondered if I was going to overdraft my account, and then figured... fuck it. She's worth it. She's that girl you only dream about but never meet in real life.

That night, we got drunk and went to some party, and despite it being almost midnight, she never took the shades off. She started making out with one of her friends whom she kept saying was hot, and I kept agreeing. She pulled me and this other girl back to a dark room in the back of this house we were in, and before I knew it, someone's mouth was on my dick and someone else's on my mouth. Then I was fucking one of them and both were moaning and there was soft hot skin everywhere. It was too dark to see anything. I could only imagine what was going on. But whatever *was* going on, it felt amazing and like there were a hundred hands and wet mouths on my body.

After I don't know how long, I heard the door open. Light crept in from the hallway. The door shut, and I lay there in the dark, my body drenched and becoming one with the bed. I wondered where she and the other chick had gone. I got myself up, stumbled around, found my clothes on the floor, and decided to go find them.

I never did.

A couple weeks or so went by, and I hadn't seen her again until I ran into her at a party on east campus. She was with someone else. She didn't have on those expensive green Wayfarers I bought her, but some light blue ones. This guy she was with looked like a total loser, but I didn't care. I was with someone else also, and this new girl I was with seemed an exact replica of the old one but only better, like she had been manufactured in the same liberal-Democrat-hates-jocks-loves-punk-bands factory—equally free spirited, if not more, and loved life just the same, if not more. And our sex... it was also out of this world. Or maybe it just seemed that way because of the drugs. Or maybe, that's just how it was with girls from the city—wild, wet, uninhibited, dirtier, different.

Better.

Despite me loving the girls here in the city, and how they so eagerly threw their inner selves at me, it wasn't long before I got tired of that whole party scene I had become a part of. And the buildings and streets and cars made it seem hotter and more miserable than how I remembered it ever being back home. I remember standing outside several hours after the sun had gone down, the salt from my sweat burning my eyes, and thinking to myself that this is no way to live.

I dropped out of the school I wasn't attending anyway and moved back home within the following week. It was hot, but not as dreadfully hot as it was in the city. I was horny, so I asked my ex to give me another chance. She did almost *too* easily. I remember walking into her parents' big house—they were out of town—and up the stairs where she was waiting. I opened the door to her bedroom. She was propped up on her bed on full display like a gift wrapped in red lingerie I hadn't seen before, and she seemed cleaner and shinier than how I remembered.

I made my way into her perfect room, surrounded by the stuffed animals she had since she was a little girl, and her perfect self was on that perfect bed, enticing me. I walked over to her. My dick was hard. I started kissing her. She said that she missed me. I continued kissing her. She asked if I had been with anyone else. I told her "No," and then thought about the girls from the city and their free-spiritedness and their wild bedroom antics and the threesome I had and said again, "No." I continued kissing down her neck and slid her red bra down and kissed on her breasts. She smelled and tasted freshly-bathed—like edible soap mixed with *Happy* perfume, which was refreshing.

I gently pushed her back onto her fluffy white bed and climbed up over the top of her. After a minute or so, our roles reversed; she was on top of me, kissing my chest. I looked at her kissing my body, her innocent crystal eyes peeking up from time to time—she was really trying to be naughty—and wondered how or why I ever left. But then I noticed this picture of her and her cheerleader friends on her nightstand. As good as her warm mouth felt getting lower and lower, I was fixated on that picture. As clear as the picture was, I couldn't tell her from her friends. They were all blonde, toned, had perfect teeth; it looked like the picture was stolen from an Abercrombie and Fitch store. They all looked...perfect. And when everyone is perfect, then everyone is the same. And being the same is only...ordinary.

I remember the way she smelled and the way her hot breath felt on my chest and then on my stomach, which sent pulses of electricity throughout my body. She unzipped my pants and worked them below my knees and kept kissing my stomach, slowly working her way down, one soft nibble at a time. She grabbed my dick and then looked back up at me and asked me again if I had been with anyone else. Then she said she had too much respect for herself to allow herself to have sex with me if I had been. I assured her that no, I hadn't. I then thought about the way those city girls smelled and tasted, and it was different.

She started kissing me again and slowly, even slower than before, inched her way closer to my dick one kiss at a time. It tickled. I remember when she stopped. I lay there for a second thinking, *What the fuck?* before looking up. Those crystal eyes were staring back at me, and I smiled and said, "What, baby?"

She didn't smile back but more scowled, her eyebrows pulling to the center of her face. Her eyes went from mine back to my dick. She moved it to the side and leaned in closer to examine something.

"What?" I asked.

That's when she leapt off me. She paced frantically back and forth, back and forth, shaking her head and looking into some distant land before calling me a liar and cursing which was not of her typical character. She told me to get the fuck out. I remember asking "What?" again and again and again, and her just repeating the words "Liar," and "Get out," and "Fuck! Fuck! Fuck!"

I left her that day in all her perfection, in her perfect room in her big white perfect house, and I remember thinking that she will someday make some successful politician type very happy.

On the way home, my dick started to itch. I scratched it, but that only seemed to make it worse. It soon turned from an itching to a slight burning. I remember that night, seeing the small red bumps and trying to pop them, but goddamn, it hurt.

The next day, my parents asked me where I was going, and I lied and said, "To a friend's." I remember thinking about the girls from the city and the threesome and thinking that not any of us, in all of it, even as much as mentioned protection, and shaking my head in disappointment at myself. *Fuck.*

I pulled into the doctor's parking lot and embarrassingly sat in that lobby for what seemed like an eternity before being escorted into a cold examination room and being told to sit up on this bed thing that felt like frozen plastic. I remember the doctor coming out, and of course she had to be female, which made my situation even worse. She asked me how many partners I'd had in the past three months and if we wore protection. I wanted to say only one, and yes, but I said, "Three or maybe four" and "No." She put on latex gloves and examined whatever those fucking little bumps-turned-blisters were that had gone from itching to burning like angry wasp venom. With a tone that was too straight and calming, she said I was now one out of four young adults, and that there were treatment options to keep the outbreaks from flaring up. She also said I would need to let any of my partners know to get checked. She nonchalantly suggested she take some blood for testing, saying that one STD could lead to another, and threw out some statistics I can't quite recall. My stomach dropped out of me.

I remember that girl from the city in all her free-spiritedness trying on those green Wayfarers, and the other guys checking her out while she tried them on, and her loving the attention. There was the threesome and then the other girl I started fucking from the city whom I almost couldn't tell apart from the first. All the girls in the city were so imperfect, they were the same. And when everyone is the same, then everyone becomes...ordinary.

I remember thinking that I wanted the fucking money back for those shades.

The doctor put on a new set of gloves and told me that what she was about to do was going to hurt a little, but it needed to be done. She squeezed on the blisters. They popped one after the other. My eyes went black. I had never felt anything so fucking venomously painful in my existence. Fortunately, the paralyzing stinging of the popping blisters only lasted a few moments, which was long enough.

Leaving the doctor's office that day, it was hot out, but not nearly as miserably hot as it was in the city. I was glad to be home.

THE APPLE

I remember the first time I saw Marie. She was out on the dance floor movin, shakin her ass side-to-side, danglin it like a ripe delicious apple, and boy, she could move. Everyone in there was lookin at her, includin the band. I think the singer may have forgotten some of the words to his own songs, watchin her. Ha. I didn't care much for that band or dancin. I watched her from the bar.

Later, she came up next to me, and she was damn good lookin. She smiled at me, and wow. I offered to buy her a drink, and that's how we met. She asked me if I wanted to dance, and I said, "No," and then she asked, "Why not?"

I told her I liked to save my energy for "other things," if she knew what I meant. She laughed, and we goofed around for a while and had a few more—*maybe twenty*—drinks.

She told me she worked for the state and had a fifteen-year old daughter, and the girl's dad was an asshole. She wished she never married him, but she was young and naïve. I told her I'd never been married, because I wasn't the settlin down type. She asked what that meant, and then how old I was—*in a condescendin kind of way*—and I asked her right back. She told me to guess, so I did. I guessed high. "Forty-five?" She slapped the shit out of me, and from that point, I knew where this was headed.

We stumbled out of the bar. I followed her home, and she told me to be real quiet goin inside. I walked in behind her, and there was rap music blarin, and it smelled like weed. There were a few kids inside drinkin, runnin amuck. She yelled at the kids to get the hell out of there and one of the girls—her daughter, Shay—yelled back, "Take your sexual escapades elsewhere!" and then yelled, "Where'd you find this one, Mom? You slut!" After a minute or so, the kids stormed out. Marie apologized to me for her daughter and asked if I still wanted to stay. I told her not to worry about it and that yes, I did want to stay. She fixed us a drink and we got after it, and I mean *really* after it. From then on out we were inseparable.

A month or so later, Marie and her daughter Shay moved into my place, because she couldn't afford rent anymore because her lowlife ex was behind on child support. Marie and me got along great, but sometimes the fights between her and Shay were out of control, almost violent. And it seemed like every fight took it a little farther. I figured it wasn't my business to step in, as I had only been datin Marie for a month or so. So I didn't.

Me and Shay didn't really talk much, with the exception of me tryin to tell her that her mother meant well and all that. The only time Shay would say more than two words to me was when her mother wasn't around. When her mother was home, Shay'd either be locked away in her room or yellin at her mother. What a mouth. She was a firecracker just like her mom. You could definitely see a younger Marie in Shay.

One day, I came home and overheard Marie on the phone with her ex. She was cryin and yellin, and I remember her tellin him she'd fuckin kill him. I figured it best to stay out of all that and that she could handle herself. It wasn't my place to butt in. This became a daily thing with them two and when she wasn't yellin at him on the phone, she was complainin to me about how he used to run around on her and call her ugly. I couldn't believe how anyone could call her ugly. She was beautiful. And then, she told me how he was abusive and how he had pushed her down. She later told me he beat the shit out of her, and after a while, she let out that he would beat her all the time. She even said she had suspicions of him molestin Shay. I asked if she had filed any police reports, and she replied, "Why? What are those assholes gonna do?" Another week or so went by, and I had had enough. I grabbed the phone and told that bastard to not ever call over here again unless he had all his child support payments written out in a check ready to pay. I hung up.

The next day, I had been workin on this roof, and it was only about 100 degrees out. You ever been on a black tar roof during summer? It's Hell's stage. I was beat... I get home and walk in and Marie is cryin hysterically, and tells me that her ex is goin to take Shay from her. She said he had record of her drug use from a while back, and that he would get custody because of it. Seein her cry like that was the worst thing you could imagine. Marie was the sweetest, most genuine woman I'd ever met. I loved her. I held her and told her I wouldn't let that happen, and the only thing she said was, "I want him dead." And at that point, so did I. I hated that no-good motherfucker.

I don't remember how it happened, exactly, but it seemed like overnight we were plannin his death, every detail. And I was goin to be the one to do it. Marie became obsessed with it, like it was a game. Anytime we were alone for five minutes, she'd go into some excited kill frenzy, tellin me exactly what I needed to do and how to do it, almost like she had done this sorta thing before.

A couple days went by. Marie was outside doin somethin, and I asked Shay what she thought of her dad. She said he was a deadbeat and then added that I was much better lookin. She was a funny one.

That Friday was the day. I couldn't believe it had come so quickly and that we were actually goin to go through with it. But every time I'd have my doubts, Marie would start cryin and tellin me all the bad things he had done to her and get me all worked up again. She'd ask me if I loved her—of course I said yes—and then she'd say that if I *did* love her, I'd do this for her. She'd look at me with that naughty sex-kitten look she did, and man, I was weak. I tell ya, men will do some crazy things for a woman like that. A woman like that has got total control. She knows what she's doin.

That night, I followed him home. I waited till about three that mornin to finally knock on his door—I was nervous. He opened and I pushed my way in and shoved the knife into his stomach. Just like that. I felt his blood coverin my hand. It was warm. That's all I can remember. I blacked out. I don't know how I got home or what I did with the bloody clothes or anything that happened the rest of the night.

With that bastard gone, I thought everything would be perfect, but before you knew it, tension in the house built between Marie and Shay and the fights got worse and worse.

I was on the couch and out came Shay in panties and a t-shirt, and she was really startin to mature, and goddamn if I didn't have to look away. She looked just like her mother, only...younger. She sits next to me on the couch, and asks, "What time is Marie gettin home?" And all these thoughts are goin through my head, and I tell her, "Will you please cover up? And it's not Marie. It's Mom to you, young lady."

She looked at me for a second and smiled and then got up and slowly strutted off in front of me toward her room. And I'm sorry, but I couldn't help but look at her ass. She was almost flauntin it like a ripe juicy fuckin apple. Before she got too far, Marie walks in and sees me on the couch and Shay in the hallway in these little panties and flips out. She throws down her purse and rushes toward Shay, yellin at her to get some damn clothes on. They go at it and I hear Marie accusin her daughter of tryin to seduce me and Shay yellin back that she is just jealous of her. After a while, Marie comes out and gives me the most evil look I had ever seen, sayin, "What the fuck, Rob? Don't let her walk around here without clothes. That's sick. She's a fifteen-year old girl." I tell her she's nuts and it wasn't like that, and that I had just told her to put some clothes on.

A few months or so go by and Marie and Shay are fightin more than ever. Both of them are always cryin and yellin, callin each other sluts and all that. Horrible names. Shay was now sixteen, and man, she was somethin. She was a hotter, younger version of Marie. Bad but innocent at the same time, just like her mother. I couldn't help but feel that she had a little schoolgirl crush on me. And Marie, the more she saw me and Shay goofin around, the more distant she became. It was like she couldn't get over the thought that I had a thing for her daughter. She knew I was attracted to her. How could I not be? But I hid it well, and I wasn't about to ruin what me and Marie had over some perverted fantasy. And anyway, I loved Marie. She was a helluva woman.

One day, Marie had to leave town for a funeral. Her great aunt had passed, and I couldn't get off work, so I stayed behind. I was watchin SportsCenter and here came Shay in these tiny little shorts and see through t-shirt. She plops down right next to me on the couch and looks at me, and with her little girly voice, asks, "What you watchin?" And I almost couldn't answer. She felt so warm next to me. I instantly got turned on, but tried to focus on sports and not her perky tits poppin right through her shirt. I mean, wow. I forced myself to look away before I did somethin stupid and told myself to *watch TV. Watch TV.* Shay then said she had to tell me somethin and went on reluctantly to say that Marie had beaten her and had done so on countless occasions when I wasn't around. She also said that Marie was usin drugs and that she had suspicions that she had been runnin around on me. She said her friends had seen her mom with some guy outside of some motel. I couldn't believe it. I asked her if this was the truth, and she stared me straight in the eye and asked, "Why would I lie? You are the nicest, coolest guy I have ever met." She then went on to tell me how I could do so much better than her mom and that her mom was a liar, a manipulator, and an abuser. An all-round bad person. And *this* is why her dad had left them, and not the other way around. Shay then hugged me close and told me she was sorry, but she couldn't keep it in any longer. I told her it was okay, and she started to cry. I felt so bad for Shay. She was so innocent and sweet, and before you knew it, her warm breath was on my neck, and it felt good. *Too* good. I got goose-bumps. Then she started kissin my ear, and I knew where this was goin. I couldn't control myself.

And believe me, I tried. We went at it, and I don't think I had ever had sex like that. Shay had some energy in her. Wild.

For the next few weeks, me and Shay would have sex every chance we got, any time Marie wasn't around. I'd leave work a little early and she'd meet me, and we'd do it in my truck. After a while, I got brave and started sneakin out of bed with Marie and into bed with Shay. I couldn't get enough of her. I mean, if you saw her, you would've done the same thing. Trust me.

Their fightin continued and worsened with time. Marie was certain Shay had bad intentions with me, and I assured her over and over again that she was goin crazy, and there was nothin bad happenin. There was definitely some jealousy from mother to daughter and the more me and Shay spent time around each other, the more distant Marie became. The house was just...awkward. You could cut the tension with a knife. After a while, I didn't want to be around Marie and only wanted to be with Shay. And why wouldn't I? Shay was a younger, hotter, sweeter version of Marie, and more full of life than you could imagine. Her energy was intoxicatin.

Soon after, the more me and Shay spent time together, the more I felt...resentment for Marie. She was keepin me from Shay. And the more those two would fight, the angrier I would get at Marie. This anger soon turned into hatred. Believe it or not, I was actually startin to *hate* Marie.

I get home from work one day and Marie's car is gone, and I get excited thinkin that me and Shay can have a quickie. I walk inside and Shay walks out of her room and her lip is busted and she's cryin, and at this point, I am pissed. Shay was so sweet and innocent. I loved her. I asked her what happened and told her I wouldn't let anything else happen to her, and the only thing she said to me was, "I want her dead." And at that point, so did I.

Within a week we had come up with a plan, and I was goin to be the one to do it. I remember tellin Shay, "I don't think we should do this." And her tellin me over and over, "There's no other choice if we want to be together." And then she'd melt me with her eyes and use her cute little girly voice and ask, "Do you love me?" and her eyes would bat at me, and I of course would say yes. I *did* love her.

She became obsessed with killin her mother and instructed me on every detail: how to do it, where to do it, and when to do it, bein now. Two days before the day, she actually had the nerve to tell me she wasn't goin to have sex with me until after I'd executed on the plan. I thought she was jokin, but she wasn't. And believe me, an ass like that will make a man do crazy things, so I wasn't about to let her down.

The time came, and I told Marie I was takin her on a date to a surprise location and that I wanted to show her how sorry I was for the way I had been actin lately. I remember her smilin and her wrinkles all the makeup in the world couldn't hide and me just wantin to slap the smile right off of her. But I held it in and went along with the plan. I blindfolded her, and we drove out into this secluded area, and that's where I did it. I walked her out into these woods pretendin to carry a picnic basket, but in the basket was a knife. I hadn't looked at her sexually in awhile, but seeing the cellulite in her legs and her saggy ass under that dress, walking in front of me— she just didn't take care of herself. Once we were completely out of view from anywhere, I pulled the knife out, covered her mouth, and stabbed her and then stabbed her again. I felt her try to struggle, and I remember shovin the blade in as deep as I could and twisting it. I don't remember anything else after that. I blacked out. I don't even know how I got home or what happened afterwards.

I woke up the next day with Shay lyin on my chest naked, and I couldn't believe I had gone through with it. I was almost...relieved. I thought to myself, now me and Shay can finally be together with nothin in our way. No evil bitch. Nothing. Everything will be perfect.

After that, me and Shay had got along great and had sex two to three times per day. I loved her more than I'd ever loved anyone in my life and despite her only bein seventeen at this point, we had a connection beyond a *normal* connection. It's like we were meant to be together. Fate. No other woman had ever done to me what Shay had done to me. Not even her mother. Not by a long shot.

Several months passed, and we figured it was best we moved to another town so we could start fresh, as bein in that house reminded both of us of Marie and all the yellin and fightin that went on. So we did. It seemed like overnight, after we got moved into our new house and Shay was in her new school, that problems erupted out of nowhere. Shay seemed distant, and before I knew it, she was withholdin sex from me, and we were fightin. I'd done everything for this girl, and I just didn't understand why she was actin this way toward me. You'd treat a dog better than she treated me.

A couple weeks passed and things got worse. Shay left for school and I found myself cryin and then feelin pathetic that a grown man was cryin over a seventeen-year old girl. How the fuck was she playin with my emotions? I'm better than that. I'm a grown fuckin man. That's when I wished I had never met her or her mother. I was doin just fine before I met Marie or Shay. But as much as I tried not to, I loved Shay.

That whole day, I had a funny feelin in my stomach, and I decided to drive up to Shay's school. I parked a block over to try and catch her comin out. That's when I saw her walk out with another boy, hand in hand. I watched her walk with him and saw him spank her ass, and saw her smile at him and hit him. They were playin around like two teenagers in love. At this point, my heart is racin and I'm havin trouble breathin. I wanted to rip his fuckin hands off. The thought of her with someone else, the thought of her havin sex with someone else, I couldn't even...

They got into his car and I decided to follow them from a couple cars back. They drove a few streets down and parked in front of this house and both got out and went inside. I pulled up and parked a few houses down and just sat there and watched, my hands tremblin. I don't remember if I was mad or what, but I had no control over my body. I heard myself breathin harder and harder and felt my heart thumpin and thumpin.

Thirty minutes or so went by and I saw the front door open, and they both walked out. I took a good look at this teenager prick's face she'd been kissin on, and he looked like such a little boy. A little pussy. I remember his fuckin face as if he was right in front of me, smilin. He couldn't be a day over sixteen. What'd she see in him? He was a pizza-faced child for God's sake, that little prick.

I don't remember how I got home, but I beat Shay there. She walked inside, and I asked her where she'd been. She told me to fuck off and she was at school, and *who was I? Her father?* She went into the bedroom and slammed the door. I didn't say anything about followin her and seein her with that fuckin little boy.

After that, things only got worse, and Shay now had nothin to do with me at all. I felt like I *was* her father, as any semblance to a romantic relationship was gone. She wouldn't even look in my direction when she was around, much less give me affection. After a while, we didn't even speak to each other, and she was hardly home. I'm sure she was with that damn kid. But if that's what she wanted, then so be it.

I remember that night. It could've only been a matter of weeks since we had moved here. Shay went out. I asked her where she was goin, and she said, "Fuck off." The door slammed behind her. I lay on the couch and watched TV for a while before fallin asleep. The doorbell rang. I looked down at my watch, and it was three o'clock in the mornin. It rang again, and I wondered who the hell it could be and then hoped it was Shay just locked out or somethin. I walked to the door, and through the peephole I saw that damned boy, the one Shay had been kissin on. My heart jumped, and before I even realized what I was doin, I unlocked and opened the door. And before I could get it opened all the way, the door pushed in and I felt a stingin, burnin pain in my ribs. I had never felt anything like that. I saw his crazed eyes lookin into mine, and at that point, I blacked out. I don't remember what happened. I just remember wakin up on top of that kid. There was blood everywhere. The kid looked like he had been butchered, his stomach cut open, almost...hollowed out...like a gutted deer.

I sat down on the floor and I could barely breathe, and that's when I felt that stingin pain in my side again.

I was in trouble. I could barely see straight, I assumed from the loss of blood. Everything looked hazy. I crawled to the phone and noticed I was holdin a knife. I peeled open my hand to set it down, and my hand and knuckles were sore from grippin the damned thing—I must have been holdin it for hours. I grabbed the phone and dialed 9-1-1 and told them everything that happened and that I needed an ambulance, but the kid did not.

Months passed and I don't know what happened to Shay. I know they were lookin for her for a while, but had no leads. Her picture was up on the news for a few days until a better story came out. She never came to visit me. She never wrote. She was gone.

I remember how her ass looked in those panties, like a ripe delicious apple dangling from a tree and how sweet and innocent she was. Despite everything, I still had hope that someday the guard would tell me that there was a beautiful young lady by the name of Shay here to visit me. At that point, I could get some answers, some closure, and move on with my life, or what's left of it. Maybe die with some sort of dignity. Or maybe she'd ride me with that tight little ass of hers like she used to. I'd fuck her as hard as I could and she'd tell me she'd missed me and would wait for me until I got out, she'd wait forever and she'd always love me, but that never happened. She never came. Shay never came. No one did.

I wish I had never met Marie. I was doin just fine before her and her daughter.

THE STORY OF THE BEAR MAN

He loved bears. That's all he talked about. He was so passionate, so zealous, almost...well, not almost—he *was* fanatical. He was an activist, a protector, a savior to them. Poachers beware! Although were there really poachers? I mean, there were enough protection agencies and law enforcement already in place to deter poaching, and there never was really any documented threat of it in this park. So what poachers was he protecting the bears from?

Every year, he would show up, construct his tent compound, and live alongside the bears. Living with the bears, according to him, was apparently something so exhilarating and magnificent, he couldn't even *try* and explain it to you; us folks who hadn't had no way of understanding. And the connection he had with them...

He'd tell you the story of how he came within ten feet of the thousand-pound alpha, and they locked eyes, and there was this connection of souls, one of the most amazing moments in his life. But you'd never be able to comprehend the feeling—the connection—withoutexperiencing it, so he wouldn't bother wasting either of your time trying to explain it any further. On and on he'd go about how majestic and caring and nurturing these beautiful animals were and how humans could learn a lot from them, speaking to you, but more so speaking to a sold-out crowd from a stage.

The questions would come: "*You are unarmed. If poachers do come, how are you going to stop them?*" And, "*What if one of the bears attacks you?*"

He'd stare into whoever's eyes who just asked the question. Unflinching, he'd say to them, "I'll do whatever it takes. I'll die for these beautiful creatures."

The guy bled passion.

"*But what if one of the bears attacks you?*"

He'd talk about this one guy out in Alaska *pretending* to live with the wolves, and *pretending* to protect them from poachers, but how that guy was doing it for all the wrong reasons. "*He doesn't really have a connection with the wolves. There aren't really any poachers. He's after publicity, fame. What an asshole.*" Then he'd show you videos he had taken of the bears, but mainly of himself ranting and raving and protesting alone in front of the camera. He looked like a one-man Broadway production. On and on these videos went, with little footage of actual bears and endless footage of his one-man show. He'd record his tantrums on poachers and hatred for hunters. Looking into the camera, cheeks red with passion, he'd build himself up into some evangelical badass, someone that shouldn't be fucked with, if they (the poachers) knew what was good for them.

His life was completely consumed by this devout love for bears that none of us other bear-less people could even *try* and understand. And when you or anyone else came within speaking range, *you'd* become consumed. It's all he talked about. And this love, this connection with bears, gave him one-up on everyone else around. He had the story that could not be matched: risking his life every year protecting bears from unseen poachers: their protector, their defender, their savior.

And for all the right reasons too, not like that asshole out in Alaska exploiting wolves for his own personal notoriety. He said he wasn't after fame or any of that and if no one knew of his selfless, courageous, death-defying acts, it wouldn't matter, because he felt it: that connection. He said if he could save one bear in all his life, then his life would be worth something. And that's what mattered to him.

He'd tell you about how he sold his story to some television network and how they were putting together a documentary on him to show to the world. He told a few others, *actually everyone in the bar*, of his newfound TV success, but how it wasn't important, and he was only trying to save bears, and if it were up to him, he could do without all the attention.

On his last trip, he took some lady friend along with him. She had been drawn in by the romanticism of his overwhelming passion for the bears, as had many. They set up a tent and filmed and filmed. The camera was always rolling. She worked behind the scenes, operating the camera, and was rarely apparent at all, more like the ghost of a production assistant than a friend or partner. Every now and then, you'd hear her giggle from behind the camera at one of his many jokes, before he'd say "Cut" and then "We'll have to reshoot." They bathed downstream from the bears, and it was amazing, unworldly. There were no sightings of poachers, although the threat was high, so he said.

The camera that recorded the audio was found a few yards from the campground. From what the officials say is, he got too close to the alpha on the wrong day. You can hear his lady friend desperately coaching him to lie down, pleading with him to play dead, and then (what sounds like) a woman screaming "Help!" and then his lady friend yelling, "Run!"

His body—only a few of his bones were left—was found next to one of his blood-covered shoes. His lady friend's body was never discovered.

He loved bears. That's all he talked about. And he died doing what he loved: protecting the bears from these ghost poachers that were there but never seen. Honestly, I don't feel bad for him or even his lady friend. Who I feel bad for are the bears. Because now, who is going to protect them?

PRETTY MEAT

Ninety minutes a day and a pretty face... You'd be amazed at what some good looks and time in the gym can do for you. The possibilities are endless: get an agent, get a role, get laid and get laid some more. Having *just* a good face or *just* a good body will only get you so far. You need both—the total package—to really make it big. This is why you eat right—no carbs after seven, keep your fat intake under twenty grams per day, no fast food—NEVER any fast food. Fat people eat fast food.

You do a minimum of thirty minutes of cardio per day, time well spent on the elliptical behind the young blonde with the great Lululemon ass who spends half her life on the stair climber. You spend a minimum of forty-five minutes on resistance training. Guys come up to you. "What do you do for this or that?" pointing to their biceps or delts that are inferior to yours. "Genetics," you reply. The face... Well, outside of a gentle exfoliant every other day (exfoliating every day would strip your face of essential oils and bacteria, actually aging you prematurely) and some retinol and collagen peptides prior to bed, you were born with that. You'll start out with a couple modeling gigs, then do a couple local commercials, then some national stuff, then land that sitcom role on *Grey's Anatomy* of a guy who dies after having a steel pipe pushed through his chest, his wife crying at his side while Dr. Yang delivers the bad news. The day would come.

You're doing standing dumbbell curls, twisting at the top to get peak contraction. You look good. Your arms have a nice pump.

"Hey," some guy says.

"Hey."

"Have you ever done any modeling?"

And that's how it starts, the gateway to the stars. This guy you thought was going to hit on you is only a talent scout, admiring your gifts. He tells you about this modeling gig that pays good-looking guys like you good money; says he's an agent.

"Here's my card."

The next day, you call the number on the card and they want you in, ASAP. You meet at this studio apartment downtown for your first shoot.

They want you in jeans, nothing else.

"Take your shirt off."

"How much are you paying me?"

"Five hundred per session."

You remove your shirt. The gay guy setting up the lighting salivates over you. It's flattering, really.

The camera flashes.

"Put your hand here."

Flash.

"Pull your pants lower with your thumb. Look at the camera."

Flash.

"Flex."

You do as they say.

Somewhere, women are going to stroke their pussies to the image of your abs, visualizing how big your cock is; what it would feel like; what the whipped cream would taste like being licked from your chest and lower abdomen.

An hour later, you put your shirt back on. They write you a check for five hundred dollars, and you're done. You feel good.

The next day, you get a call.

"You received a lot of views. They want you to do some full nude shots."

"Wow. That's great, but no thanks."

"They'll pay you a lot for full nude. Plus, this will look great on your modeling resume. And anyway, you know your body's made for it."

"I don't know."

"A thousand dollars a session."

You take the offer. You meet at the same apartment building. The same cameraman is there, but with some different guy working the lights. There're also two other guys hanging out. One brings over some vodka.

"Here."

"Thanks."

"And this will help take the edge off."

He hands you a Valium that you swallow.

"Disrobe."

You take your shirt off.

"How much do you work out?"

You explain your workout routine to the guy that has never seen a body so sculpted.

"Your pants."

The shoot begins.

Flash.

"Put your hand here."

Flash.

"Turn around."

Flash.

"Turn back around."

Flash.

"Stroke it."

Flash.

"Keep stroking it."

Flash.

You think about all the women that are going to cream their panties looking at pictures of you stroking your dick that isn't huge, but bigger than average and still impressive. Thinking about this makes you hard. All the guys in the room are fixated on your gift of a body.

"Okay," the cameraman says, coming up from behind the camera, breathing heavily.

One of the guys hands a robe to you. He eyes you up and down.

"Nice work."

The way he said that makes you a little uncomfortable. You quickly wrap the robe around your waist. You slide your jeans up over your legs, drop the robe, and put your shirt on.

"Here you go." They hand you a check for one thousand dollars.

"Thanks."

You leave feeling shameful about your decision to do the shoot, but then think about all the women out there toying their pussies to your photos.

The next day, you get a call.

"You received a *ton* of views. They *really* like you."

"I'm sure."

"They think you've got what it takes to go next level. They're talking movies."

"Movies?"

"Yep."

This is it: your big break, and it's happening practically overnight. It's amazing what a pretty face and 90 minutes a day in the gym will do for you

"What kind of movie?"

"Well, porno."

"I don't know."

"What do you mean, you don't know?" All of a sudden this guy gives you attitude.

You give some back. "Look, man, I don't know."

"This is your big break and you don't know?"

"Well, yeah."

"You already showed your dick to the world."

And despite how grand this sounds, you don't feel good.

"And now they want to pay you two thousand per scene to show it, and you don't know?"

"Two thousand?"

"Yep."

That's a lot of money for fucking some hot chicks while women everywhere masturbate to you.

"Do I get to pick the girls?"

"Girls? There are no girls." The casual tone of his voice scares you.

"I don't get it."

"There are no girls. This is a male-only movie."

"What?"

"Who do you think you've been stroking your cock for?"

This is where you realize it isn't women that want to see you, it's men. Practically overnight, you've become a hit in the gay community, receiving the most hits on some dude-on-dude site. Your stomach drops out of you. *Why didn't you see this? Why didn't you question them?* You hang up on the words coming from the other end.

Over the next couple hours, the phone rings several times. You don't answer.

The next day, that hot blonde with the great Lululemon ass is at the gym, getting off the stair climber. She smiles shyly at you.

You smile back. "Hi."

That night, you take her for drinks and then fuck her back at your place.

THE COMPLEXITIES OF TIME AND WHAT NOT

That boy was obsessed with time. I mean, really, *obsessed* isn't even a strong enough word.

I was a friend of his dad's, the boy's. Me and Jimmy worked together at the town mill back in the seventies, and boy, did we get into our fair share of trouble, let me tell you.

I remember one time, we left work and met up with a couple girls at The Dust, that ol' bar down on Harpers Lane. You ever been there? Anyway, we're having a good time, I mean a *really* good time. The shots are just flyin and next thing you know, we're stumblin out of the bar with these girls, drunk as skunks. There's these fellas out there waitin for us, and they're pissed. But we don't know who these boys are. Then one of 'em tells me to get my (pardon my language) damned hands off his wife! I say, "Wife?" And before I know it, I get a fist in my teeth. I'm dropped. When I come to, I see the boy's dad, and he pulls me up and drags me to the truck. On the way home, I notice blood on his hands and shirt. I ask him, "What'd you do?" And ol' Jimmy says, "I took care of 'em." I say, "Both?" And he says, "Yeah."

That boy's dad...Ain't nobody mess with him. He didn't look like much, but he'd fool ya.

The years passed and Jimmy met this girl, Betty, and she was somethin'. She looked like a young Marilyn

Monroe, and boy, did she know how to wear a dress. They dated for a spell, and after a while, that lucky sombitch—sorry bout that—made an honest woman outta her at that ol' Baptist church off of Springdale Road. I hate that they tore down that pretty little church and built that new shopping-mall-looking one. But you know how those big-wigs and fancy city folk are. They don't give a damn—pardon my language—about what's right. They only care about what's big and new and shiny. Like greedy little rats.

Anyway, before long, Betty had the boy. She was an absolutely beautiful young mother, but Jimmy...he didn't seem all that happy as he shoulda been.

I'd come over to drink some beer with Jimmy, and Betty would have on one of those form-fittin dresses, and boy, could she wear it. She'd bring us beers, and I'd sneak a peek at her behind when she'd walk back inside, and man. One time—ha ha—she turned around, and I was caught! But before I could be embarrassed, she just smiled at me and it's like my world stopped. I didn't know what to think of it at the time. Anyway, me and Jimmy would sit there and drink beer and talk about this and that and what not, and he'd complain about the boy and about Betty. Meanwhile, she'd bring us out ice-cold beers before we'd get to the last sip of the ones we were holding. It's like she knew exactly when we'd need another one. And the way she wore that dress...I'm sorry, but I don't know how she squeezed that little boy outta her.

The boy was a baby at that point, but before you knew it, he was runnin around and gettin into trouble like any normal boy that age. I don't know what his first words were, but I bet ya anything they were about time. He was obsessed with it. He was a bit...*different* upstairs, if you know what I mean, too smart for his own good. While most kids were still shittin themselves—excuse me—the boy was already readin about time theory, and speed of light, and other fancy science stuff. That boy, I tell ya, could take a watch apart and put it back together in less than a minute, and that's when he was only six or seven. He was somethin, alright.

Betty would buy him cheap watches from the Dollar General off of Whitehelm St—it's still there—and let him play in his little time-fantasy world. His dad didn't care much for his interest in all that.

I remember one time, we were having our beer on the patio, and Jimmy told him, the boy, "I don't wanna hear another Goddamned—pardon my language—thing about this time travel bull! It's stupid!" I remember the boy running off crying and then the look on Betty's face. I felt bad for her and wished I could comfort her. All I wanted to do was protect her, but I couldn't.

The boy got older, and Betty—don't get me wrong—still the most beautiful woman I knew, was starting to look tired. I went over one day, and she came out with beers for me and Jimmy, and that's when I saw it: a busted lip and a black eye. I couldn't believe it! I couldn't believe he hurt her, that sombitch. Excuse my language. The beers certainly didn't taste as good as usual that night and Jimmy didn't have much to say, and neither did I, because how the hell could someone hurt a woman that beautiful? We both just kinda stared out into the night. At this point, the boy, who must've been ten years old by now, didn't even come outside no more. God knows if he had been hurt, too. I left that night scared for the both of 'em.

A couple days later, I went by the house to check on the boy and Betty while Jimmy was off at work. Betty opened the door and saw me and started looking around me all wide-eyed and worried like. I told her I just wanted to make sure they were okay and assured her that's *all* I wanted, and that's when I saw the boy. His arms were covered in...bruises and his nose was busted and he, too, had a swollen black eye. I couldn't believe Jimmy had gone this far, the bastard. Sorry about that.

The boy walks up to me, his eyes stuck on my watch, and asks, "Are you late, Mister?" And I say, "Late for what?" And he doesn't tell me. He just walks back down the hall. His mother looks at me, her teary eyes begging me to save them. And boy, did I want to just hold her right there and squeeze her tight as I could, but that wouldn't be right. So I left, and this is where it gets really tricky. I couldn't allow another bad thing to happen to that woman or that boy. They deserved more than that. But I couldn't confront Jimmy, cause he'd do me like he done them other fellas.

That's when I went down to the Speedy Mart off of ol' Oak Street—you know the one—and made the call from the payphone. Told 'em I had information on the death of two young men back in seventy-four that happened in front of that ol' bar: The Dust, off of Harpers Lane. They knew the one. They asked what kinda information, and I told 'em, "I know who did it. I know who killed those men." I told 'em the story, and then they asked for my name, and I got scared and hung up. Not scared of getting in trouble with the law...but scared of what Jimmy'd do if he found out who told 'em.

Within an hour, they arrested him at the mill where he still worked after all those years.

I went by that evening to check on Betty and the boy, and she answered the door, asked me in, and offered me a beer. I obliged. She cried and cried, but I could sense some relief on her part, like she was finally safe. I held her. That was the first time. I squeezed her and let her cry on me, and I wouldn't let her go, and boy, did she feel good. The boy was there, but in his room, his mother said, working on a time machine. Her and I drank a couple beers and talked, and I told her how I was sorry to let that sombitch—excuse me—do that to her and the boy, and I would never let another bad thing happen to her or that boy ever again. And that was the first time we made love. And boy-oh-boy, the years had done her right. She was more than I coulda ever dreamed of.

As years passed, Betty and me never got married, but we were happy together, and I tell ya, she just got more beautiful each day. The boy went off to some big school to do some fancy science stuff, and Betty and me bought a nice little house off of Mulland Lane. You been there in a while? It's a nice area. Anyway, I remember the boy and his obsession with time and how he'd always ask me, "Are you late, Mister?" And he'd never tell me what for, and finally it occurred to me. Maybe I *was* late. To what, I don't know. But maybe we are *all* late to somethin.

It was sometime in September when the school called Betty and told her her son had gone missin. We drove into town—I hate drivin in town; it's almost unrecognizable with Chinese restaurants and apartments and too many people. I remember when these streets were lucky to see a car for hours... Anyway, we put up flyers and asked everybody we could if they'd seen him. No one had.

Once the detectives had gotten everything they needed from his room, evidence and what not, they allowed us in to collect his stuff. Everything was still there: his clothes, his wallet, a half-eaten pizza. It's like he just...disappeared. He had prolly twenty clocks that he had taken apart and put back together in bizarre shapes and sizes scattered all over. There was contraptions, and pipes, and gears. It looked like a...factory or somethin. There was a...ammonia smell, or the smell of cleanin products, but I didn't see any evidence of no cleanin.

We gathered his things. Betty broke down when she picked up an old picture of him and her and his dad. I grabbed hold of her and squeezed her as tight as I could. I told her everything was gonna be okay and that we'd find the boy, although for some reason deep down, I knew we wouldn't.

Weeks passed. The police called and asked if we wanted to come pick up some of the boy's blueprints or drawings—I forget what they called 'em—and I said "Sure" and asked what they were blueprints of. The officer said they looked to be of some designs for a make-believe time machine and then all these writings of time theory, multiple dimensions, a bunch of other fancy science stuff I wouldn't know the half about.

The next day, I didn't want to bother Betty with anymore of this seeing how hurt she was, so I told her I was gonna go to the hardware store and drove back down to the station. I met up with this black officer fella who had called—I think his name was Johnson—and he got me the boy's stuff. I asked about the case, and he told me they had some good leads. Said they believed the boy had gotten mixed up with the wrong people and been involved in drugs. I couldn't believe it and told him they had to be wrong. But the officer assured me they weren't. He said that they hadn't ruled out abduction, because all the belongings left behind fit an abduction, but they thought there was also a good chance he was over in Mexico cookin drugs. The one thing they couldn't figure out, he said, the one thing...there was no forced entry, and the door was locked from the inside. I asked if maybe the boy climbed out the window, and he said, "Nope. The window was locked, too. Plus," he said, "he was on the third floor with nothing to climb out onto."

We both decided it best not to worry Betty with any more of this until they knew for certain where the boy was. She had been through enough. So as far as anyone was concerned, me picking up the boy's belongings that day never happened.

I tell ya, I don't know about any of what the police are sayin. But I do know I got these plans—or I think they called 'em blueprints—of some machine that I think you might want to take a look at. You're a business man, and that's why I'm telling you all this. I don't have the means to make anything happen—I'm just an old man— but you do. That boy was obsessed with time and time travel, and I tell ya, I think he found a way—the only way—and I have it just sittin here, ready to give to ya. But it's gonna cost ya.

THE LOOK

John's face is tense, his eyes staring off at nothing.

"I…"

There's a quiver to his voice as he shakes his head side to side, staring downward, looking deeper into that nothing.

"I…I don't know."

Smoke rises from the cigarette that he's holding but not smoking anymore. The ash is growing and leaning. For some reason, I can't take my eyes off this ash that hangs on by a thread, teasing me, mocking me. *Fall, motherfucker. C'mon. C'mon!*

"I mean," John keeps on, "I thought *this* was our last resort."

His hand hasn't moved, but when it does, that fucking ash is coming down. I feel my anticipation growing. Blood pumps through my heart more viciously, my body on high alert. *C'mon!*

"It's like plan A and plan B went out the fucking window."

He's still talking on about whatever, but I all I can think is, *move that hand, John. C'mon, you mother…*

"And now we're stuck, man. I…I don't know what the fuck to do."

The ash finally falls and for some reason I feel a sense of relief, but really don't understand why, and then get thrown back into reality and our situation at hand. I look up at John. His eyes are piercing me.

"Dude," John says. "Are you fucking here, man?!" He taps his temples firmly with his index fingers, pointing to his brain. His jaw is tense, teeth grinding, his eyes now impaling me.

"Uh, yeah, man. I'm here."

"Good. You fucking better be. You are in on this, too."

Hearing the words "in on this too" makes it hard to breathe for a second, before I snort a small laugh.

John stands up and starts pacing frantically back and forth, saying, or more like pleading with no one, "Aw, man. I've got a fucking wife and family." His voice cracks, which is so weak it's annoying. I can practically hear the tears.

He covers his mouth and looks at me briefly before turning back around.

"I've got a little girl," he says choppily, each word getting stuck in his throat before being broken loose.

He looks at me, his eyes like he's seen a ghost, his lungs swelling, his head tilting back, chest out and in. I can now *see* those tears I thought I heard a second earlier beginning to run onto his face.

I've only seen that look once before—that look of complete and utter fear and desperation-turned-despair. Actually, I remember seeing a program on Discovery a while back about these lions in Africa or wherever and they chase down this...I don't know...wildebeest? The young wildebeest gets separated from his herd and surrounded, and after a valiant effort to escape, there are simply too many lions. The lions close in around him and claw and swipe and bite at his legs and trip him down, as he kicks and bucks and does everything in his power to survive...*really* fighting desperately for his life. After a long while, probably several ten-or-fifteen minutes, they finally get him down all the way. There's four or five of them, and they claw into him and keep biting his legs, pulling him this way and that way, gripping and tugging on his arms or legs or whatever, and this wildebeest is just tired, having expended all his energy, all his reserves—every last ounce—and there's just too many. He knows what's coming next, and you can see the sadness in his wide-open eyes, a look of total hopelessness. Not desperation, because the time of desperation had long passed, but just...hopelessness, despair, as he gives in and rolls to the side, accepting his cruel fate. You can see the drooling lions reflected in the helpless wildebeest's giant, dark, almond-shaped eyes as they bite into him and start tearing away layers of his flesh.

That look... the same look John has now.

So I guess I've seen that same look now...three times?

John sternly grips my arms and turns me to face him, his eyes flooded, his mouth sagging, his hands shaking, his nails penetrating through my shirt and skin and says more intensely than anyone has ever said anything to me, "You. Are. Fucking. In. On. This. Too," wrapping his mouth around each word to further enunciate what he's trying to imply. His nails dig deeper into my skin.

"Yeah, man, I fucking know! I know!" I laugh.

He releases his grip and stands up tall and straight to compose himself and slowly backs up from me, removing his eyes from mine after a few seconds. He looks off at nothing again and resumes pacing.

He paces slowly for a few seconds more, pauses, then kicks the bound girl on the floor in the stomach as hard as he can. She'd cry out, but her mouth is duct-taped. He kicks her again.

"You fucking cunt!"

Small whimpers leak from her sealed mouth.

"And you!" He points at me. "You wanted a fucking hostage. This was your fucking idea. And for what? So you could fucking rape her? Well, you got what you wanted."

John paces frantically again, stops, and peers at me. I can't keep from chuckling.

"It was a simple robbery, and now"—he pauses to compose himself—"we have a witness to our little crime. Fuck!" He yells at the sky.

"Calm...the fuck...down," I tell him, leaning further back in my chair, getting more comfortable.

John shakes his head in disgust, huffs, and leaves the room.

The girl's eyes are fixated on mine, locked, and have that same look of hopelessness that John and that wildebeest had had from that show—that look of hopelessness. Of weakness. And I think that this one certainly didn't give up as easy as that wildebeest, or nearly as easy as John, and it was only till she had been tied up, gagged with tape, beaten relentlessly, then violated from behind over and over again until my dick was too raw to go on—because *what else are you going to do with her, now?*—did her eyes shift from a begging desperation to hopeless despair.

With John in the other room, I get out of my chair and lie down on the ground in front of the girl, staring into her eyes.

She starts crying behind her taped-up, muffled mouth. Her wide-open eyes are pleading with me, desperately searching for any morsel of human compassion left inside. But there is none.

"Shhh," I tell her.

I pet her head—her hair is wiry and matted—and look around as if I'm being secretive, ensuring my partner is in the other room and can't hear.

"It's all over. I'm gonna get you outta here."

Her frightened eyes eventually close and tears of relief flood out of her and down her cheeks to the floor as she whimpers and cries. I can only imagine how she feels, thinking that she is going to survive, that I am going to *let her* survive.

"It's okay. Everything's gonna be okay."

I place my thumb and index finger over her nose, softly squeezing, closing off her air passage. Her eyes open back and, panicking, she tries to thrash about, but she is bound and exhausted, so her movements are short and weak, her eyes begging and begging. It's amazing what a little bit of false hope can do. I keep her nose squeezed shut, holding her head firmly in place with my other hand, grasping tightly onto her hair, as her final fight comes to a close.

I think to myself, *this one had fire.* She just took it and took it and took it. The way her ass resisted my dick before blood finally lubricated it... My dick hurts just thinking about it.

After what must be thirty seconds or so, her begging eyes staring deep into me, pleading, her desperate look shifts again into that oh-so familiar look of hopelessness. And then, after one last, final, unsuccessful attempt to breathe and a concluding kick, or spasm, or more like a jolt, pulsing from her abused, failing body, her look of weak hopelessness transitions into...acceptance. Her body goes limp.

"See? Good girl. It's all over," I say as I softly pet her head.

Her eyes, still locked on mine, are now emptier than they were before. All I can see is my smiling face reflected in them. I smile back.

WORDS, MISERABLE FUCKING WORDS

It's raining out. Raindrops are bombarding the windows. Hundreds, thousands of bullets pound to get in. There's an occasional deep rumble accompanied by a flash that leaves you seeing spots, and then the rumble subsides softly. You hear the relentless barrage of water bullets coming from every direction, encompassing you, your world. The windows, the walls to the right and to the left and in front of you and behind, the roof above you. You are trapped and under attack, left to wallow in your thoughts, which is far worse than death. It's really coming down.

The blinds opened, only thin cream-colored see-through drapes hang down over the windows allowing you to see the darkening manic sky outside: at one-point turbulent, then peaceful, then turbulent, and then peaceful yet again. Then comes the growl-turned-roar of thunder and a bright flash and the spots, all of which hit fast and hard and then subside softly.

It's not cold inside, but you feel cold, damp. You take a sip from your coffee and listen to the rain. The coffee is not as hot as it once was, only slightly warmer than the air. Besides the sound of the rain, the thunder, and the occasional spontaneous flash of lightning, there is nothing. No sound. Nothing. Just you sitting at your really-not-big-enough-to-be-dining room table in your dark apartment listening to the rain, sipping on your coffee, contemplating your next line to her. You tap the point of the pen to the pad.

Tap. Tap. Tap.

One lamp with a low-watt bulb blankets your apartment in a soft yellowish glow, enough for you to see but not enough for you to see well. There's a low rumble, and your world rattles, a bright flash and then those spots again, count 'em: one, two…ah, they're gone. Throughout, the sound of the rain continues, steady.

You take a sip from your dying coffee and the longer it sits there, the worse it tastes. The longer you sit there, the worse you feel. It's cold, but more of an internal cold. The apartment's not cold. It's you. Your bones feel chilled, wet, how you remember feeling when you were a kid coming out of the pool and going inside, entering a house with the AC set at 68 degrees on a hot summer day.

You feel the rush of arctic air hit you as you slide the glass door to the side and reluctantly enter. Your trunks sopping wet, the tile floor is like ice on the bottoms of your feet. Droplets fall from you onto the tile as you speedily tippy-toe to the bathroom to change from the freezing wet trunks.

Then a rumble shakes the apartment, and your bones and apartment windows rattle, and there's a blinding flash outside and then the spots, one, two, three…and they're gone again.

You drink from your decreasingly warm and increasingly bitter coffee and set it down, and it tastes worse than before. You feel the pen still held in your right hand. You squeeze it and roll it between your thumb, index, and middle finger, absorbing the hexagonal shape. You sit there listening to the constant rain, which sounds so rhythmic and so…steady, it's like…nothing. You contemplate. Hmmm. What do you say to her? How do you tell her what you feel? You've never been good with words. You're not a writer. You don't read. You don't even talk well. Actually, words have always been more detrimental for you than beneficial. If you could go without using words at all, you'd be better off. You wouldn't be in this *how do you say? Predicamund?* If there was a way to retract words after they were spoken, then that would be something. If you could un-say words after you've said them. Words. Fucking…words. Words, or more like, *your* words, have always got you in trouble. They've ruined everything you've ever *almost* had.

Your not-even-really-lukewarm-anymore-coffee ripples as the apartment shakes from a furious rumble accompanied by another startling flash and then the spots, one, two, three, four and…they're gone again. Besides the steady beating of the rain and the incandescent soft yellow light from your low-wattage lamp, an occasional grumble of thunder and strike of lightning, the fleeting spots, your rapidly cooling half-drunk coffee, and this cold feeling, it's just you. Just you sitting there reflecting on what you did, on what you said, what words you used and mulling over what *to* do, what *to* say and what words *to* use. If you could only un-say words. *Fuck.* You tap the pen-point to the pad—*tap, tap, tap*—but not intentionally; it's just your muscle memory like an anxious robot controlling your body. You hate fucking words, but you know that despite words historically being your downfall in more than one…hundred occasions, you know they are your only chance at salvation. Your only chance to, *how do you say? artriculate* how you feel. What you feel. And what do you feel? What the fuck do you *really* feel? Not just externally, but internally. And not no bullshit-teenage-lust-shit either. The real shit. The real love. The kind of love where you still want to be next to her even *after* you fuck her. Do you *love her* love her? Like that? Do you?

Crash!

A loud roar startles you, along with the flash of lightning and the spots, one, two...and they're gone. You take a sip from your on-the-verge-of-being-cold coffee, and the sound of the rain blankets anything and everything. It feels like the walls are closing in around you, the room getting smaller, and you sit there and try to determine what it is you need to write and what it is you even *want* to tell her at this point. Do you love her? Actually, do you *like* her? Because you obviously don't love her, or you never would have done what you had done. *Right?* There's no way someone can treat another person that way and do what you did if you *love them* love them. You physically wouldn't be able to. You physically wouldn't be able to say those things. *Right?* Yeah, right. You wouldn't. Your heart wouldn't allow it. You'd be, *how do you say? imcabable* of hurting someone if you truly loved them, if you truly loved her.

The storm is calming and the rain has lost some of its force, but is still a steady, consistent downpour.

Maybe you never loved her. Maybe you thought you did. But maybe you didn't. Maybe it was just the excitement of being with someone new that disguised itself as love. Maybe that's what it was. Maybe that's what it *is*. And what is love? Does love even *really* exist? Are we capable of love? Capable of, *what's the word? cumpastion* beyond...*comprassion* for our own selves?

A low growl penetrates your world with a quick flicker of white through the window and through the apartment, and there are no spots this time. The storm is moving. The worst is over. The rain is still constant but dissipating.

You are more confused now than you've ever been, but maybe that's because you had a breakthrough. A, *what's the word*? *Etiphany*? Maybe you never loved her. Maybe you've never loved another human being, ever, in this life. Maybe you will never love another human being. If you are not capable of loving, are you capable of being loved? And now this is a whole other can of worms. Maybe you don't have to love her to be with her, to have her love you back. Maybe that's the only way. Maybe she *was* the closest you've been to loving another human being you'll be able to reach. Maybe she is. *Fuck.* What the fuck do you say to her? What do you write? There's no way for you to take back what you have already said. *Is there*? A way to *un-say something*? You are holding the pen with the point touching the paper, tapping it, tapping it. The rain is softening and becoming sporadic. Through the windows is becoming lighter. The yellowish tint in the apartment is becoming more...grayish. And you have it. You have the words! The words! You now know exactly what words you are going to write! And so you do.

Dearest Erica,

I haven't been completely truthful to you or myself. But today, I had a breakthrough. Finally, for the first time ever really, I see the light. Sitting here, listening to the rain, has made me see what I couldn't before, and this is exciting news for both of us! I now know why we would fight and why I would say such hurtful things to you. Erica, my dear, I never loved you! Never! And I think I was trying so hard to love you, or anyone for that matter, that it was driving me crazy and making me push you away. And that's why we fight, and that's why I say such unspeakable things to you. And now, I can let that go! I can be ME and be with you, and you can love me, and I can be happy with NOT loving you! Please call me as soon as you get this! I know you changed your number, but I will be waiting by my phone! I miss you dearly and can't wait to see you! I'm so excited for what tomorrow will bring!

Sincerely...

LOVE THY NEIGHBOR

"Yes, Dad," I say, but have no idea what incessant mumbled words are coming from the other room over the TV that is a continuous stream of Fox News set to volume eleven.

Outside, there's some squealing from a heavier vehicle in need of new brake pads. I pull the blinds. A large white moving truck is parked along the curb in front of the house with the sold sign and there's a black Jeep, and getting out of that Jeep is a... *Holy moly.* I feel my lungs empty and my cheeks heat to volcanic proportions, along with the deep tribal drumming of my heart *pumping, pumping, pumping.* My hand gravitates to my crotch that is begging to be touched. I gently rub it, trying to satiate the tingling sensation, my cock expanding, imprisoned by my pants and briefs as I watch this little vixen with hair as dark as space itself and eyes like blue electricity that can be seen from lightyears away, and those legs... My mouth falls open and my tongue reaches for her scent, pulsating as if it's alive and thirsting for her, yearning to paint every inch of her body as if possessed by Artemisia herself. I close my eyes, imagining those heavenly legs wrapped around my face with my tongue lapping at the sweet, sweet salt from her vaginal walls, my nose buried between the pink flaps as she moans and moans and pulls my head in farther and farther, and *oh fuck.*

The tingling becomes rapid-firing electric jolts that consume my entire epidermis and turn me into a spasming statue, unable to move even as the hot bullets turn to ice on my thighs. As the sensation subsides, I open my eyes. The girl—the girl that I must have—is now gone, replaced by the geriatric couple across the street who are working in their yard, *always* working in their yard. I instinctually release the blinds and back away, hoping the girl I have never seen before but have dreamt of my entire life didn't just watch me fondle myself and ejaculate—a little *too* quickly, I might add, because I can last more than sufficiently when it's called for.

More unintelligible grumbling comes from the back room that smells of Ben Gay and onions.

"Yes, Dad. Be right there."

***

I watched for her, telling myself that I would go outside and introduce myself to this beautiful, stunning, erection-inducing girl next time she came out, but the only three times she's made an appearance so far— *reclusive, mysterious, sexy*—weren't the right times. Of course, my stomach had been upset once from the microwave meatloaf, and the other time the VCR went haywire as usual, always at the worst possible moments. *Technology.* I thought the clunky thing had eaten episodes six-oh-seven, oh-eight, and oh-nine of Disney's *MMC*, which would've erased the timeless television moment where Ryan, Britney, and Christina got their asses handed to them by a drill sergeant. Thank goodness, it hadn't. You can't find wholesome, quality variety shows like that on present-day cable television. The MMC delivered a feeling, made you a part, made you feel like you actually belonged to something, like you existed. The last time she came out, she walked with intensity, obviously preoccupied with something, weighed down by some impending meeting or task, on a mission I simply could not interfere with.

Each rare sighting of her invoked that fluttering butterfly thing—*cliché, but who cares?*—that I had only experienced two or maybe three times in my entire life—the series premier of *Xena Warrior Princess* and then again with *Ocean Girl*—but never as strongly or as real as this.

Our first meeting has to be perfect. It must be. Our futures—our lives—depend on it.

Since her arrival, there are no signs of any roommates or house guests, or husbands, which bodes well for the middle-aged, intelligent, classically handsome neighbor. A woman like her needs a strong, confident man, someone to help around the house, carry her groceries, mow the lawn, protect her, bite her tender back while he cums inside her asshole. I'll be that man. She'll see. In the beginning, I'll worship her. But in the end, it will be she who worships me as we embark on a love story that transcends all others, like a god and goddess amongst a world full of inept and powerless nothings, everyone and everything around us nothing but props in our eternally running television series.

I pull down the blinds expecting and hoping to see her Jeep and those legs leading up to that black dress that's cupping her ass like two ripe melons, but she has been gone now for—my watch reads nine forty-two—two hours and thirty-seven minutes. *Where are you, my little bunny?*

The old man from the other room—the curse from the tomb—beckons me.

"Yes, Dad. I'm bringing it now." I carry the barely-warm TV dinner of Salisbury steak and corn down the hall and into the room, my mind racing. *Where could she be?* The thought of her with someone else, eating French fries with ketchup—*I wonder if she says catsup*—laughing, smiling, falling for his dirty tricks with his perfect sandy-blond Kevin-Sorbo-Hercules hair and biceps, devaluing herself just enough to suck his cock that is the same shade of tan as the rest of his body... *No!* My lips purse, and air forcefully exits my nostrils like a bull sizing up this sculpted half-God, half-man rodeo clown who spends every waking moment in a gym or tanning bed, a man *she* is too good for—WAY too good for.

I bring myself back to the present, and Christ Almighty, the smell of rotten onions, of impending death, seems to grow more pungent by the day. I look at my dad, now more age spots and bruises than brittle, pale, translucent skin. He says something through labored breaths. His lungs and throat strain, working hard to get the words out, but the mucus in the back of his throat dampens the enunciations, and the lack of teeth prevents the sounds of consonants, every word strung together like a one-note song from a droning zombie. I just nod and smile and hand him his food.

"Be careful. It's hot." I say that almost mockingly, considering the steak is probably still cold in the middle, which is more than he deserves, the old codger whose eyes haven't left the TV and its continuous news cycle for years. I nod, feigning interest in the silver-fox broadcaster sitting above the rolling headlines, but can care less about this degenerate world which is all death, pornography, and sadness: Satan's playground.

I walk out and pull his door closed within inches and hurriedly get back to my post. Through the blinds, I see headlights and then the Jeep, and *there you are. Wait. Who the fuck is this guy?* The blond statuesque Kevin Sorbo comes to mind, but no. Some dipshit asshole climbs out and walks around the Jeep, clumsily stumbling over his clunky feet, his wide, soft frame bouncing off the vehicle. This guy isn't even fit, which, although it shouldn't, annoys me. And what's with the suspenders and beard and pants that don't touch the tops of his shoes? "Come on, my bunny. This guy?"

She grabs his hand and smiles at him, which punctures my heart before leading him up to the house. *No. He isn't right for you.* This sheik who somehow travelled from the roaring twenties is practically raping her with his eyes, salivating like a disgusting dog, tripping over his two-tone oxfords, high-fiving himself and ready to tell all his scumbag hipster friends about tonight's conquest which is just that for this guy, another fucking conquest, and I guarantee he hasn't read more than thirty books his entire life and is mentally and emotionally bankrupt with nothing to offer except that stupid fucking beard and hard-part with greasy pomade. I'll never understand how any woman—especially a goddess like this one—could have such poor taste and judgment. My knuckles hurt from my tightening fist, and I want to pulverize this inauthentic imbecile, beat him to a bloody pulp, but I can't. That would not be the best first impression. And anyway, I'm not some primitive ape who can't control his impulses, unlike this grimy, suspendered, pea-brained cave-dweller motherfucker. *Fuck! Fuck! Fuck!*

I step back from the blinds, accepting the realization that this slimeball's greasy hands will be all over her perfect body and his small pecker will be doing no other than the infamous jack rabbit—a wham bam thank you ma'am—and then he'll sleep like the coward he is, satisfied, while she lies there unsatisfied, looking down at this pile of overdone garbage and regretting granting him the right to her body, her pussy hot and throbbing for something good, something only I can give her, while a single tear slowly works its way down her cheeks and jaw, a tear that I can taste. I stroke myself, gripping harder and harder, willing myself to hold out until *she* cums, because my satisfaction comes from *her* pleasure, *her* moans, and then we cum together in a sticky wet mess that smells like the honeysuckles in my grandparents' yard I used to suck on as a kid when I'd be left there all day with no one to play with.

***

I try to sleep but can't. All I can think about is her with this imbecilic loser, and just the thought makes my face twist like a contortionist and heart send blood to my extremities and glucose to my brain, this feeling of utter helplessness almost unbearable. I get out of bed; there will be no sleeping, tonight. And anyway, the average American only sleeps for two hundred and eighty-three minutes per night, so catching up over the next seven days would only require another...forty additional minutes per night, which is basically two commercial-free episodes of *Ocean Girl*, which makes me think of Neri, which arouses me a little but not enough; Neri is old news and been-there-done-that for the last thirty years.

There's a cough from the other room that is louder than usual, which means he is closer to death but still alive. I peek in on the weak bag of bones that used to be strong and forceful and drunk and violent, his eyes closed and lips quivering from the minimal amount of air his lungs still take in, the faint whistling becoming fainter with each day. That stench—the smell of dying cells—lingers on the air like a toxic fog. *It won't be long.*

"I'll always hate you," I whisper, pulling the door closed as quietly as possible, swallowing back the acid that tried surfacing, and walking back to the front window.

I twist the blinds just enough, pull up a chair, and watch. The waning gibbous moon is providing high contrast over the street and the homes that feel colder and lonelier than normal. *Where is she?* I notice my heel tapping from anxiety, which only sends more cortisol through my body. I clench my fists and feel my hands wrapped around this loser's neck, constricting until the carotid is cut off and numbness and dizziness overtake him, the lack of circulation making this bearded, suspendered dullard more stupid than he already is. Again, not the best first impression, but what happens inside my head doesn't necessarily have to come to fruition. I'm beyond that; better than that. I've trained my parasympathetic nervous system and amygdala to resist fight, flight, or freeze. I've evolved, unlike this overly-groomed Neanderthal. I've had to.

I watch and wait, continually checking my Timex, until finally after three hours and fourteen minutes and almost a full box of Twinkies and two glasses of Ovaltine, she reveals herself, but *where is the cumsack?* This dark-haired Goddess, whom I can only imagine smells of Heaven and sugar, is struggling to drag a large—*is that a trashbag?*—down to the curb. The muscle fibers in her calves and thighs are working, tense, her glorious ass in the shortest thin cotton shorts I've ever seen contracting, up and down. The thought of the sweet sweat between her legs, between her rubbing ass checks, leaves me no choice but to expose my member that is throbbing to be inside her, and it only takes a couple of strong tugs before an explosion of tension is released. When I open my eyes, she is gone. *Until we meet again. Next time will be the time.*

***

It's another two days before I see her again, and she is down the street before I have time to wipe the shine from my forehead and comb my hair. *Always in such a hurry.* "Where are you off to, now, my princess?"

One hour and forty-two minutes later, she is home, and this time with a guy that looks twice her age, even older than me, drunk and swaying, following this goddess into her castle, and now I'm at a loss. *Another man? Why are you doing this? Why? What the fuck does this aging nobody have to offer you with graying hair and saggy balls and baggage from several ex-wives and a flaccid worn-out cock? Is it some red convertible he drives to compensate for his lack of intelligence, his lack of humor, his lack of stamina, his lack of commitment? Why, bunny? This dirtbag isn't good enough for you, not by a million light years. Fuck!* His dry hands are probably already all over her smooth, warm body, her supple breasts, her lips on his, her tongue dancing with his... My dick gets hard, and I stroke it angrily until her eyes stare into mine while that old bastard rams her from behind and my body convulses as goopy strings fly onto the floor, and at this moment, fuck the floor. Fuck everything.

***

A little after three a.m., she comes out in a one-piece satin nightie that is made for her body, accentuating every curve, every contour—*I wish I was that nightie*—with no sign of the older guy who is probably named Terry or Tom, something ordinary and boring, *and is that...another trash bag?* The petite vixen is walking backward, struggling to drag yet another large black trash bag that must double her weight down the driveway. *What are you up to, my bunny? What are you disposing of?*

I sit and stare out, my mind circling the thought that I've seen two men go in and no men come out.

She leaves the cumbersome bag on the curb for the trash men that should be by within the hour and walks back inside. *Two men. Two large trash bags.*

It can't be, right? I mean, I've read about these kinds of things, and there's no question Satan has his grip on the world these days, but can it be? I look at the trash bag and yes... you could fit a body in there if chopped up correctly: the torso split long ways and limbs cut into twelve-to-fifteen inch chunks. I instinctually recoil from the window that separates me from fresh human remains and stand there lost in some bizarre nightmare where my future wife, the mother of my children, is some kind of murdering psychopath.

Two nights later, another drunk asshole enters but only a bulky black trash bag leaves.

***

Why is he stopping? "Don't stop." This boy, who must be only nine or ten, sits on his bike like the king of naïveté, talking to this monster while his dad is drunk and his mom is on autopilot, going through the motions, setting the dinner table, unaware of her child's whereabouts and wishing she was anywhere but there.

"Why'd you stop, kid? Just go!"

Now the kid's laughing, and *what is she telling him?* He climbs off the bike. "Don't do it, kid. Don't fall for it. Go home! Please!"

The older couple across the way are working in their yard—always working in their yard—not even looking up; the world could end, and they wouldn't look up—*Goddamn it! Look up!*—as this poor, stupid boy walks his bike by the handlebars, following behind this *thing*. The bloodthirsty temptress turns back and smiles, which makes my stomach flip over and acid rush my throat. "He's only a child, Goddamn you!"

The vixen disappears into the house—her cave, her lair, whatever disgusting thing you call it—and this boy— this poor, lonely, unwanted child that looks a lot like me when I was his age—is only steps away from being inside with her—three steps, two, one.

"No, kid!" I bang on the window, knocking the blinds crooked, as he vanishes from view. I press my palms over my eyes as hard as I can, smothering my oily face, and grip what little hair I have left. My whole body trembles as I pace furiously back and forth in a red haze of confusion and anger, and *I can't just sit here and do nothing. I can't. I—I have to do something, but I'm scared. I'm always fucking scared.* "Come on, you cowardly poltroon." I slap my face repeatedly, fire spreading across my cheeks with each shot.

Not anymore. Every moment of my pathetic life has led me to this point in the universe, and this time, I *will* do something.

I slide on my shoes and pull the Velcro tight. My dad mumbles something between loose, phlegmy coughs.

"Not now, Dad."

I twist the doorknob in slow motion as my heart pounds, desperately trying to escape this cage of anxiety and paranoia. My hands shake as I push the door open, and...

***

The old man, Ned Pearson, had been dead for months, his skin practically rotting off, and the smell... Of all my years on the job, I had never walked into anything like that. We found three more bodies on the property: Mr. Pearson's wife and daughter, the third body an unidentified male in his early-to-mid thirties.

Ned Jr. kept on about the new neighbor girl across the street, who he claimed was killing people and chopping them up, and went on and on asking about the boy on the bike, seemed genuinely worried. But the Pearsons didn't have any neighbors. There was no one around. The only house within a quarter mile of theirs had been abandoned for years. Ned Jr. obviously wasn't fit to stand trial and was shipped off to that big ol' mental hospital upstate, you know the one.

I tell you, that smell... like pure death. You never forget something like that. That sorta thing lives with you, haunts your dreams. Well, until it's your time to go, and you do the haunting.

MY FIRST TIME WITH JESSIE SPANO: A FLASH PIECE

I remember that first time: the feeling of jumping from a scorching hot day—the cement burning the bottoms of my feet—into the refreshingly cold depths of the neighborhood pool. I lost my breath as I hit, before ascending to the surface, breaching that barrier and taking a deep breath mixed with the splashes of overly chlorinated water.

I was twelve, coming on thirteen. Those curves, that wavy long hair, those lips... Looking at her tall womanly figure made my dick tingle, the end feeling like a red branding iron pulled from the fire. I was just a hairless kid *barely* on the verge of pubertic greatness, but there was something about her, something I didn't quite understand and still don't. I wanted her. I wanted *it*, whatever I dreamed *it* to be. I didn't know what or how, but I knew.

Growing up watching Jessie Spano on *Saved by the Bell*, years went by without this feeling and all-of-a-sudden came this relentless sexual thirst for her. It was new. It was different. I remember the first time I felt it, rubbing and stroking my adolescent member now newly engorged with blood—picturing her bare skin—and the insides of my body exploding, sending millions of tiny needles shooting out of every pore like how the sun would feel, my entire body tingling, before leaving a hot-turned-icy plaster on my upper inner thigh.

After that, I longed for that feeling and did whatever I could to recreate it, by this point several times a day. Every chance I got, I would close myself off and picture Jessie Spano and what her naked body would look like and feel like: her taste, her smell... I could hardly handle it.

It wouldn't take more than 30 seconds of imagining her before the canals would open up and the molten river would run through it and onto the land and into the ocean: the sink, the toilet, a towel, my shorts.

Each time, I came close to reliving that first robust time but never could quite get there, and after several (about thirty) sessions with Jessie, my want and need sadly moved on. My teenage self had become bored, complacent. My desire soon shifted its way to Kelly and oh, she was a dirty girl with that fat ass and those green eyes begging me to fuck her. And I did, real good, at least inside my horny teenage mind. But sadly, even the great Kelly Kapowski became just another been-there-done-that fantasy, and with each time I imagined fucking her came less excitement.

From Kelly, it became anyone: the next-door neighbor, my mother's friends, the girls at school, the teachers, the pictures on the celebrity magazines my mother left out, the blurred porno channels. But nothing lasts forever and as the years went, so did the fantasies. With each masturbatory session came less and less satisfaction. Yes, the physics were still there, the hot sun and icy water, the taste and burning of chlorine, the tingling of my skin, although not as intense... But no matter how hard I tried, I was never able to recreate the exhilarating feeling of that very first time.

When college came, my hopes were high. There was surely a girl within the masses of young women roaming the campus. Surely.

There was Melody, who was tall and leggy but whose hair wasn't long enough. There was Laura, who had long wavy hair that was a little too dark. She was Hispanic and shorter than I would've liked and a little too curvy. Then there was Tonya with an "O," who was tall and had long wavy hair, but not enough hips. Then came Brooke, whom I thought I was going to marry. She had long wavy hair, legs that reached Heaven, hourglass curves... I often said she looked like Jessie Spano, which she found cute at first, but seemed concerned with the comparison by the time we called off the engagement. She really did look like Jessie Spano, even talked like her, but she wasn't. I pictured Jessie every time I bent her over, trying to will it into reality, but I just couldn't.

Twenty years of chasing, through multiple women and relationships and one called-off engagement, I'm still searching but for who or what exactly, I don't know. With every new increasingly disappointing sexual escapade, whatever *it* is seems to get farther and farther away. Melody, Laura, Tonya—and who spells Tanya with an O?—all these girlfriends who aren't *it*, no matter how hard I try, become disappointed in me, frustrated with me, while I'm the one whose needs and desires are being left unfulfilled. Who would've thought women would be so selfish and lacking empathy while refusing to acknowledge and correct their own inadequacies?

I don't know whatever happened to Jessie Spano. But sadly, I know there will never be another.

LOVE AND SADNESS AND FADING MEMORIES

"He means well," Joann says. "He's just..." Her voice falters with uncertainty, her eyes looking off and down. She wants to believe what she's saying, but doubts permeate her mind.

"He's a good boy."

This wasn't the first time Joann had been questioned about her grandson's whereabouts. This wasn't the first time Sheriff Stephens had been called out to this house.

"Well—" The Sheriff had heard this song and dance before. "Okay, ma'am. If you see him—if he comes home—tell him to give me a call or come down to the station and find me. I don't want this to turn into some big ordeal this time. Okay?"

"Okay, Sheriff. I will. I'm sure there's just some misunderstanding."

The sheriff tilted his brimmed hat to the old lady, and he and the other officer walked from the house, the wooden steps creaking with each step down. He opened the door to the police car and looked over to the young officer, shook his head, and laughed a little under his breath. They got in and pulled away.

Poor Joann had a hard go of things lately, especially since Herbert passed away. She missed that man every minute of her existence.

She recalled the first time he asked her out on a date. She was working the bank teller line and he was making yet another deposit into his account, an obvious excuse to see the brown-eyed girl behind the counter. He always waited for her, politely refusing to be serviced by any of the other ladies. She called him up.

"Hi, Herbert," she said and smiled, warmly.

"Hello, Joann. Can you help me with this..." he stalled, realizing how obvious he was with the second of his twice-daily deposits of a few dollars, if that, his all-too apparent attempts to see her as frequently as he could. "...deposit?"

Joann smirked, eyeing Herbert in his military uniform. He was strikingly handsome yet boyishly cute with his dithering. She had been waiting for him to make the move, hoping *this* time would finally be the time and not just another shy disappointment. Her heart raced with anticipation. Fluttering butterfly wings tickled the insides of her tummy.

Looking off, Herbert mumbled the words, "There's that new James Dean movie playing over at the Ritz. I was wondering... if you might want to go see it sometime."

Although she had been anxiously anticipating this small-but-giant moment and had gone over all the different scenarios and words to respond a thousand times, she was caught off-guard by the moment actually coming to fruition. It took her a second to catch her breath before playfully saying one of the lines she had rehearsed over and over again, "Well now, Herbert, are you asking me out on a date?"

His eyes finally met hers. He smiled a little, growing more confident and nodding his head yes, before second-guessing himself. "Yes. I mean...that is...if you would like to."

Joann tried to hold onto the memory as best she could, but she couldn't quite see the sincere eyes on that young handsome clean-shaven face of his anymore, the memories of Herbert and their life together becoming hazier by the day, seemingly getting farther and farther away. The longer he was gone, the more he disappeared, everything about him—his facial expressions, his scent, his presence—dissolving in time. The thought of losing him hit her hard. The thought of losing the memory of him was unbearable.

Joann's grandson Jesse was all she had left since Herbert's passing. She and his grandfather had adopted him after his mother—their daughter Patricia—all but abandoned him. His father was a Mexican who worked on cars—a greaser, one of those guys that wore a leather jacket and drove an obnoxiously loud car. Patricia was only sixteen, and this guy had to be close to thirty. They never liked him much, which they expressed to their daughter, which only pushed her more forcefully into his arms.

Once she got pregnant—almost seemingly to spite her parents—the greaser vanished. He was gone, nowhere. And she was heartbroken.

Patricia and the baby stayed with Joann and Herbert, and the baby brought in a newfound energy and vibrancy to the aging couple. They offered to watch him at every chance they got, which Patricia took full advantage of. Before long, she was never home, staying with some bandito she met at the bar, or so was the word around town. The visits and phone calls became more and more sparse. Patricia couldn't care less about her child, not to mention her parents, whom she wholeheartedly resented for reasons unknown. Joann and Herbert always did the best they could; they were at a loss for their daughter's callous behavior and thoughtless actions. They didn't raise her to be *that* way. They taught from the Good Book and were good church-going people. It just didn't make sense.

Time passed, but Patricia's irresponsible behavior didn't. Joann and Herbert decided, after the countless bouts of unanswered prayers that their daughter would make a turn for the better—that somehow Jesus would find his way into her heart and she'd all-of-a-sudden want to be a mother to Jesse—when all hope had faded, to pursue full legal guardianship of the boy. Patricia didn't put up a fight. To her, this was a blessing. She would finally be rid of the hindering annoyance she had given birth to and be able to live. And just like that, she was gone and no longer carrying the inconveniently heavy burden of being a mother.

Joann and Herbert did their best with the boy, but the ways of raising children had changed over the years. Life was different now. There were just as many bad paths as there were good, and it was harder for many to ride the straight and narrow. Jesse, knowing that his grandparents were older and naïve to the modern injustices of the world and felt sorry for him, used this to manipulate them. As he got older, pulling one over on his grandparents became second nature and a daily practice.

There were problems in school they were often called down to discuss.

"Jesse hit another student."

"Well, he must've been provoked. He's a good boy."

"No ma'am. He was the instigator."

At thc age of twelve, Jesse was caught breaking into his friend's bedroom to steal his action figures. He had used a large rock to break the window and gain entry. The parents of the friend didn't press charges, but did ask Joann and Herbert to pay for the broken window, which they gladly did.

Three years later, he attacked an older gentleman who was known to carry wads of cash on him and have cash hidden throughout his house, due to his openly loud mistrust of the banking system. Jesse bull-rushed the man from behind as he carried groceries into his home, knocking him and the paper bags of victuals to the floor. Several TV dinners, a pint of vanilla-bean ice cream, and some canned beans flew out across the entryway. Jesse pulled out a gun.

"Please. Please," the old man pleaded, his hands shaking as he opened his wallet and offered up the few bills that were inside.

"Shut the fuck up, old man."

Jesse counted the thirty-six dollars he snatched from the man and shepherded him throughout his housc, demanding more money, the end of the gun prodding at the old man's back, the cold steel like ice through his thin skin. Jesse became frustrated after the old man repeatedly told him he didn't have any more. Jesse turned up every mattress, becoming more irate by the minute. He ransacked every drawer in the house, slinging clothes and other items to the floor.Holding the gun pointed directly at the man, Jesse's face was red with irritation-turned-anger. He felt his hand holding the gun trembling and his trigger finger tightening.

"Put the gun down!"

Jesse turned to see two officers with guns pointed at him.

"Drop the gun, NOW!"

He did as they instructed and lifted his hands above his head before being vehemently manhandled to the ground, his hands roughly cuffed behind his back.

Jesse wasn't the sharpest tool. He didn't account for the neighborly eye-witnesses of the incident, nor the amount of time he stayed in the house rummaging for the non-existent money. Successful robberies are those that happen quickly, which he was yet to learn, learning never his strong suit. He was charged with armed robbery and aggravated assault but, being that he was only fifteen, was sentenced to a light six months in juvenile. His juvenile felony would stay on his record.

Over the years, Joann and Herbert grew accustomed to the police stopping by their house with questions regarding their grandson. Every time, no matter what the accusation was, Joann and Herbert would defend their innocent-but-misguided grandson.

"Robbery? No. It can't be him. He's a good Christian boy."

"Burglary? Oh no. It must be someone else."

"Assault? Jesse would never hurt anyone."

Joann and Herbert just couldn't wrap their mind around the idea that their grandson had somehow become a criminal, a common street thug. *How could such a good-hearted boy get steered so far off the righteous path?* Jesse might have stumbled into trouble, but he had always meant well. He had a good heart, they told themselves. They came to the only conclusion they could, which was they were poor parents to the boy, not giving him enough attention, support, freedom. Love. Already feeling sorry for Jesse for never knowing his father, or really his mother for that matter, their sympathy toward him was only elevated by their self-blame.

As the years went by, Herbert's aging body started going downhill. It seemed he was in the hospital every other week those days, and was consuming copious amounts of prescription medication.

Jesse woke to Herbert talking from the other room about the lawn needing to be mowed. He rolled over in bed and looked at the clock reading 12:13 p.m. Fifteen minutes later, he came out of his room.

"Grandma, Grandpa, I've got a job interview to get to." He grabbed a piece of toast from the counter and crunched into it. "Grandpa, I can help you with the lawn tomorrow, if you want." He said this knowing that his weakening grandfather would mow the lawn today. It had needed tending to for the past couple weeks, the blades of grass and weeds reaching up to almost knee-level.

Jesse was great at offering to help out, and was even better at finding excuses of why he couldn't at that particular moment.

The sun was going down. Jesse showed up back at the house. There was alcohol and pot on his breath. He noticed the yard newly trimmed.

"So what'd they say, Jesse? You get the job?" Herbert asked.

"What's that?"

"The job, Jesse. Did you get it?" Herbert had a hopeful smile, but those smiles didn't curl up as much as they once had.

Shrugging it off, Jesse replied, "Nope. They don't hire felons."

This little bob-and-weave went on for a while until Herbert had talked to an old friend of his who knew a guy who owned a small bricklaying business and needed some hands. Jesse's felony was of no concern to them, and therefore couldn't be used as an excuse. Jesse worked as a helper—he had no choice—for barely a week before his back gave out, which prevented him from being able to do any physical labor going forward.

When Herbert died, Jesse soon began dealing drugs from the house. Joann—still naïve and unaccepting of Jesse's darker side—just thought he had a rough-looking group of friends, in and out all the time, leaving empty beer cans and bottles scattered throughout the house. There was one in particular she didn't care for. He was dark-skinned, had tattoos, and always had a cold, blank expression, or as she put it: creepy eyes. She asked Jesse to not bring him around anymore, but he jokingly dismissed her request.

"Grandma, Jack's a good guy. Don't be crazy."

There was never a moment of peace in the house, the quiet old lady outnumbered by obnoxious grifters. Joann was forced into one side of the house while the hooligans played their loud degrading rap music and went on drunkenly on the other. As much as she didn't want to admit it, she had become a captive in her own home. She'd tell herself: *Let the boys be boys. Let Jesse be Jesse.*

* * *

It was the day of her and Herbert's anniversary. It would've been their forty-eighth. Joann awoke and looked into the mirror at the aging, wrinkled, thin-skinned, age-spotted old lady she had become. She thought hard about Herbert proposing to her in his car overlooking the hillside, only two months from their first movie-date. She couldn't quite see his face; couldn't quite hear his voice. This saddened her.

She opened her jewelry box, looking for the modest ring Herbert used to propose with. Back then, there were no two- and three-carat diamond rings—normal working folks couldn't afford them—and her three-quarter-carat was more than enough. Anyway, Herbert's love and commitment were more valuable than any diamond on Earth. She fingered through her jewelry—some necklaces and bracelets, earrings—noticing that the box seemed less full than she had remembered. She removed the items, placing them on her dresser, separating them, delicately searching for her ring. It was nowhere. *Where could it be?* She searched through her drawers, hopefully, but deep down, she knew there was no other place she kept her jewelry. It was all in the box, including her engagement ring. Her gut told her it was that tattooed, dark-skinned boy with the emotionless expression. She knew he had stolen it.

Meanwhile, Jesse had become on a first-name basis with the manager of a pawn shop a town away. There, he took tools he "inherited"—Herbert's tools—and jewelry he was "left"—gold, silver, three-quarter-carat diamond engagement rings. This extra cash provided drugs and booze for him and his friends.

Joann told Jesse some of her jewelry was missing, and again told him to keep that Jack guy out of their home. She just knew he had gotten in there somehow and taken it.

"Okay, Grandma," Jesse said, snickering. "If it makes you feel better. But I'm sure you just misplaced it."

The lawn had made it through winter and was now beginning to wake up. Green patches were breaking through the brown and spreading. Joann indirectly mentioned to Jesse that the grass needed to be taken care of, passively hinting to him that he ought to mow it.

"Oh, Grandma, I'd mow the grass, but I can't do anything with my back. Why don't you get one of those kids from down the street to do it?"

Again, he was great at offering to help and even better at finding excuses of why he couldn't. Apparently, his back wouldn't allow him to do anything other than boozing and hanging out with his degenerate friends.

Joann hired a nice teenage boy from down the street to mow the lawn once a week. He did a good job. The yard looked healthy and green again, groomed, which reminded her of Herbert. He had always given them a nice lawn up until it became hard for him to take care of it.

***

Joann finished supper—pot roast and potatoes—ate, and then retreated to her bedroom, escaping the noise and clatter of the boisterous young people who had infiltrated her home. Jesse had a friend over and a couple of young girls. One of the girls reminded Joann of herself when she was young—big brown eyes and an infectious giggle—full of life and without a care in the world. She thought back to the good old days when she and Herbert were wild and free, and the thrill of being together consumed them.

Jesse and his friend and the girls—one of them a sixteen year-old, brown-eyed, dirty blonde-haired cute girl who lived down the street, named Elizabeth—did a few lines of meth while taking shots of plastic-bottle whiskey in between. Despite the girl being only sixteen, she was mature (meaning sexually active and uninhibited, full of issues stemming from childhood abuse) for her age, and Jesse was not the least bit concerned about their age difference. He was in his early thirties, but immature for his age and horny. He fucked her for the first time that day and every day thereafter. The two became inseparable. Elizabeth was in love with Jesse, and Jesse was in love with her flawless sixteen-year-old body.

She'd come over to the house.

"Hi, Joann. You look very lovely today." Elizabeth was always so sweet and polite. She hugged Joann warmly every time she saw her.

Joann would blush and dismiss her compliments, but it did make her feel good, even if the young girl was fibbing.

Elizabeth was always eager to help Joann out around the house, too. She'd offer to do the dishes and then actually do them, unlike Jesse with his excuses. She'd help with supper, and even take out the trash. She was a giving person, a hard worker. She was a good girl. Joann oftentimes thought of her daughter Patricia whom she seldom talked to, and when she did, it always felt forced. It was good to have that female figure around the house, perhaps a positive influence on Jesse. Maybe she was the one to get him back on the righteous path. Joann enjoyed having Elizabeth there.

"Bye, Joann!" Elizabeth said loudly to Joann, who was in the other room.

Jesse finished guzzling his beer and set the bottle on the entry table. "Bye, Grandma. Be home later."

The two of them staggered from the house. It was starting to drizzle. Elizabeth walked up to the passenger side of the car, waiting for Jesse to be a gentleman and open the door. He walked right around her and opened his door and got in. He unlocked hers after a few moments, allowing just enough time for the cold rain to saturate her clothing.

She climbed in and sarcastically said, "So chivalry *is* dead, asshole." She sniggered.

Jesse peeled the tires of Elizabeth's mother's blue Chrysler Concorde on the slippery pavement as they drove off.

***

Joann got the call around nine o'clock. She was just settling down for bed, watching her detective program.

"There's been an accident," the man said. "Your grandson is in critical condition."

Joann got dressed and raced down to the hospital in the Buick sedan Herbert bought before he passed on. He loved that car, spending hours inspecting the body, wiping down spots normal car enthusiasts wouldn't have noticed. He kept that car shining like a trophy he worked his whole life to earn.

***

Joann rushed inside the hospital, eyes wide, thoughts racing, her heart pounding up against her fragile chest. She was directed to the appropriate area, passing a few police officers in the hall. Jesse was unconscious, lying in the hospital bed, wires and hoses leading to machines that beeped softly and consistently.

One of the nurses filled her in on what had happened. "He lost control and spun off the road, hitting a tree. He suffered a couple broken ribs and a concussion." She stared at Joann. "He was lucky."

Joann wondered how those injuries made him "lucky."

"The young girl who was with him may not make it," the nurse told her.

Joann couldn't believe those words, her brain not knowing how to decipher what was said. Her vision turned gray and blurred, and her knees gave out. The nurses caught her and sat her down in a chair.

"Do you need some water, ma'am?" One of the nurses—a male nurse—raced from the room to get her some water. He came right back with it. Joann drank it down and caught her breath and composure.

"You okay?" they asked.

"I—I'm fine." She recalled seeing the empty beer bottle on the entry table as she left the house. *Oh, Jesse...* She shook her head as disbelief and disappointment battled for position. *What have you done?*

After a moment of blankly staring off, Joann came to. "I need a phone."

"Yes, ma'am. Right this way." The male nurse gently helped her up and over to a telephone.

She dialed her daughter. It rang and rang. She thought she heard someone pick up before the dial tone took over. She redialed. Busy signal. She tried again. Busy signal.

Joann hung up the phone and stayed by Jesse's bedside for a while before one of the nurses encouraged her to go home and get some rest.

"He'll be fine," she assured her.

Joann stood up, her legs weak and wobbly, and walked from the room. She thought about that young girl with the big brown eyes and sweet smile. "Can I see Elizabeth?"

"We're sorry, ma'am. Only direct family is permitted."

***

Joann lay in her bed, tossing and turning. Despite her extreme emotional exhaustion, she didn't sleep a wink.

The next day, she crawled from her bed, fought to get her clothes on, both the bed and clothing more ornery than yesterday. She put on some decaf coffee. She sat there in her empty house while the coffee dripped and sputtered. She stared out into the golden day, bright with sun and life and fading memories.

There was a knock at the door. Patricia, she thought. She opened it to see Sheriff Stephens and another officer.

"Miss, Harbough...may we come in and talk for a moment?"

"Sure. Is everything okay? Is Jesse okay?" She opened the door to allow the officers in.

"That's what we want to talk to you about." Sheriff Stephens sighed and looked directly into the elderly woman. "Jesse's fine. That's not the problem. The problem is"—he paused—"is that young girl is dead because of his drinking and driving."

Joann deflated. She felt like someone punched her in her abdomen, knocking every ounce of air from her lungs, the life from her body. She could see Elizabeth's innocent brown eyes clearly. *That poor girl. That poor sweet, sweet girl.*

"There were also drugs in his system—methamphetamines."

"No." Joann shook her head, looking off and around, her eyes eventually making it back to the sheriff's. "Jesse drank, but he *never* took drugs."

Sheriff Stephens huffed slowly and then got straight to business.

"Have you seen him? He snuck out of the hospital, left his lines dripping onto the floor. Was gone before the nurses realized. We figured he may have come here."

She shook her head, her eyes again wandering as the color in her face drained at the thought of that poor girl being gone forever, dead.

"Ma'am?"

"Oh. No," Joann said. "He hasn't been here."

The last time the police came looking for Jesse, he had climbed out of the window, hitching his way to a friend's house a town over, creating a small-but-chaotic manhunt and turning the town upside down.

"Miss Harbough, we don't want any trouble this time. I really don't feel like spending my man-hours searching for Jesse. We've been through this. He needs to come down to the station and turn himself in. I've got more important things to tend to."

Joann was for the first time out of excuses for her grandson. She had spent the last thirty years defending him. There was nothing left. She wondered how such a good person could find himself in so much trouble and so often. Questions circulated through her head: *Why did bad things always happen to good people? Why, God? Why? Why must you put your people through these terrible tribulations? What are you trying to prove?*

A single tear seeped from her eye. She was broken and beginning to question her previously resolute faith. This doubt was unfamiliar and left her in a state of confused dismay.

The officers left after Joann assured them she would tell Jesse to turn himself in if he were to show up.

The next evening, she heard some rustling coming from the other side of the house before the front door opened and closed and a car driving away. By the time she made it over to the front window, the street was empty.

****

It was the day of Elizabeth's funeral. Joann got dressed accordingly and noticed the light on her answering machine blinking. She pressed the button.

"Mom, I heard." There's a sigh. "You and Dad never taught him right from wrong, and *this* is what happens." Said under her breath, "I can't even believe this shit." Pause. "You've raised one helluva winner there, Mom. Well done." *Beep.*

Joann attended Elizabeth's funeral. It was a bright fall day full of sun and life and fading memories, memories of a young girl who had fallen in love over many lifetimes. On her way back to the car, Joann stopped for a brief moment, catching her breath as walking felt more like an all-out sprint as of late. She stared at the blue sky, and swallowed the harsh reality that she was alone and there were no do-overs in this game of life. All was gone but the mistakes. The mistakes carried on forever.

She got in Herbert's pride and joy and rolled the windows down as he often did on a nice day like this. She gripped the steering wheel as tightly as her bony fingers could, knowing his strong, loving hands had once been there, thinking about the drives they would take out into the country with no specified destinations. As long as they were together, where they were going didn't matter. Images of him grinning and looking over at her, his eyes full of love, weren't as clear as they once were; they didn't stick as long as they once did. As much as she tried to hold onto the moments, she just couldn't.

She pulled out of the parking lot and down the street, passing the shops and restaurants that had changed many times over the years but somehow stayed the same. Her left arm hanging outside of the car—Herbert always had his arm hanging out like that—the sun's golden radiance broke through the cool dry air, softly warming her skin. She had felt that same sun on her skin for over eighty years. Only now it was accompanied by a cold sadness she knew would never fade, unlike the memories of a time when she was happy.

AND THE DAY SEEMED ENDLESS

He had been walking for hours. His bare feet were sore and bruised, pummeled by different shapes and sizes of unforgiving rocks. Some were jagged, some round, but either way, both inflicted pain through the middle of the bottom of his feet. A shooting pain right in that tender part of his foot—directly above the heel in the anterior arch—catching him off guard each time, as that's not something one can get used to. There was a slight breeze blowing from somewhere, *he couldn't tell where*, but it felt nice on his face and on the back of his ears and neck, almost comforting, but not quite.

He had been at it for hours—*or could it be longer?*—walking in a single direction. Not north, east, south, or west, but simply...straight. He had no idea where he was, no idea where he was going to nor coming from. And with the cloud cover, he had absolutely no conception of where the sun was to even try and determine a directional path. He stopped and looked back for a moment, feeling the loose gravel under his toes and the *almost* comforting breeze. Behind him was an exact replica of in front of him, which made him second guess his initial, instinctual choice. Did he choose the right path? It was too late for him to turn back, as he hoped to get to somewhere—anywhere—before sundown. *Which was when?* he pondered.

When he woke up however many hours ago—*or could it be longer?*—he had no recollection of where he was or how he had gotten there. He was lost, abandoned, left for dead, left to die alone out here in this boundless cornfield. And what the fuck was he doing here anyway in the middle of this Goddamned what-seemed-to-be endless cornfield in the middle of Goddamned God knows where?

After several minutes—*or could it be longer?*—of fighting this initial shock of surprise and bewilderment and elevated blood pressure and scattered anxiousness accompanied by irritation-turned-anger-turned-rage... then several more minutes, *or could it be longer*, of yelling out the words "Help!" and "Anybody out there?" then repeated failed attempts to jump high enough for his line of vision to clear the tops of the corn crops, he got a hold of himself, like *really* calmed himself and urged himself to think. *Think. Think. Think.*

Out of breath at that point but at least thinking somewhat rationally again, he figured he must choose a path: this way or that way. So he chose *that* way and began on his quest for becoming found. What seemed like hours—*or could it be longer?*—went by. Without a watch or cell phone or any other method to tell time, he had not the slightest idea how long he had been out there. Stopping to look back every now and then—the scenery the same coming or going—he had no idea if he had made any progress toward getting out of there, or getting anywhere for that matter. *How many miles is this Goddamned cornfield?*

He recalled a movie he once saw as a child about this haunted cornfield where innocent little kids were tempted to enter into it by something supernatural. Inside of it, they'd be devoured by these bloodthirsty, demonic crops, their blood being sucked up into the roots, their high-pitched screams lost somewhere in the fields. He felt a rush of chills cover his arms, his legs, his entire body. He only watched that movie once in orders of his older brother to avoid the sissy name calling that went along with "pussying" out. Once was enough. That movie provided him with recurring nightmares well into high school and into his freshman year in college, where he had awoken in cold sweats on more than one occasion, his heart pounding from his chest, his lungs not cooperating. The symptoms were diagnosed as night terrors by the doctor, which he was told was a giant step up from ordinary nightmares. Dr. Freece said these terrors were spawned, not by a supernatural bloodthirsty-fictitious cornfield, but by something much deeper, perhaps unrealistic pressure from his parents or problems in school. But Dr. Freece had never seen the movie, so he had no idea how scary it was. And until his doctor did see it, he would go ahead and self-diagnose his night terrors as a result of that movie, not no stupid problems at home or at school. Dr. Freece didn't know what the hell he was talking about. That evil Goddamned cornfield movie *was* the culprit. He hated that fucking movie with a hatred stemmed from an absolute fear of it, and his detestation grew and grew inside of him the more it infiltrated his mind like an invasive fucking parasite. He fought to keep those images out of his head and even after years of not seeing it, that movie still snuck back in from time to time, and still gave him the heebie-jeebies. To this day, every time he saw a cornfield, he got an uncomfortable uneasiness under his skin which pissed him off, because that feeling just would not fucking go away.

Of all places to wake up in, he thought, *a Goddamned cornfield.*

Something made him gasp and jerk to his right. He peered into the ocean of swaying stalks and leaves but saw nothing.

He did his best to mentally block the images of the cannibalistic corn plants tearing and peeling through skin, devouring flesh and bleeding poor little kids and himself dry, leaving only the membrane, bones, and clothing behind. *Keep going*, he told himself. Plus, he was an adult now. He knew the difference between real and fake, reality and make-believe. *And anyway*, he tried to assure himself, *the plants would've eaten me already if they were going to.* He eyed the endless plants suspiciously and shivered at the thought of having his skin stripped clean before convincing himself there was nothing in that field that was going to eat him.

The little bit of soft breeze felt nice, and he couldn't place its direction. At once, it seemed to blow at him, and then away from him. Above, the clouds were swirling like watercolors that were alive, rhythmic and melding into different colors and shapes, not moving in any clear direction.

After a while, he turned back to see what seemed almost identical to what he had seen earlier and then turned ahead. He couldn't tell the two apart, coming from going. Hours and hours upon hours went by as he continued walking, taking soft, careful steps onto his more-bruised-with-each-step feet, cringing as his soles and heels made contact. The day and his surroundings seemed endless, still, empty. "Where the fuck am I?" he asked aloud to no one, before telling himself to keep his cool, and to just keep walking.

On this journey to who knows where, scenes from his life began to slowly play through his head. He remembered learning cursive in elementary school and how proud and excited he was that day to tell his mom, jumping out of the school bus before the door was fully opened all the way, the sun and wind on his face, Transformers lunchbox swinging in hand. He then recalled being a teenager, maybe eleven or twelve, realizing for the first time the sheer sensation and pleasure of ejaculating. But unfortunately, that time, his pants absorbed the bulk of it. He remembered his first kiss in junior high—seventh grade, to be exact—outside of the town's movie theatre, and then his first pussy encounter behind that movie theatre where he finger-banged the same girl less than a week later. He remembered his first penetration with that girl less than a week after and how scared and nervous he was. He stole the condom from a convenient store and had no idea how to use it, or even unwrap it, so they cut it open with scissors. She stroked him off and put her mouth on there until it got hard, and he unrolled it down over his undeveloped, adolescent shaft. He felt like such a badass wearing a fucking condom, a bonafide fifteen-year-old badass. He remembered his first beer and how cold it was, and how it didn't taste *that* good, but he drank it anyway to avoid being called a pussy. He remembered the first time he smoked pot and recalling that pot wasn't anything he had hoped for, but besides the coughing, it was alright. So then he tried lacing it with coke, and that was better. He remembered his buddy Ryan's mom: Miss Toungate. He'd sneak over to Ryan's house during school hours and fuck his mom after snorting coke with her, and he thought about how good it felt and what it smelled like afterwards. He could still smell it, which made his dick twitch. He remembered one time, hauling ass out the back door when her husband (Ryan's dad), pulled up in the driveway early from work, and having to remove his dick from her insides but not wanting to. He ran out of the gate and down the street as fast as he could until he got to his backyard, where he tried to catch his breath and compose himself before entering his house. He remembered the guns Ryan's dad owned and had leaning up against the wall in almost every room of the house, and thinking to himself that he should be scared but wasn't. He continued fucking Miss Toungate (but at that point he called her Susie) every chance he got. Their affair continued. He wasn't in love with her, but he was in love with the excitement and the adrenalin fueled by the magnitude of how undeniably wrong his actions were and the possible repercussions: loss of a close friend, split marriage, broken household, soured reputation. He never once tried to justify what he was doing, because there was no justification. If there were any smidgeon of a reasonable excuse, the excitement— the fun—would be lost.

Their affair continued even into college and survived not only her marriage but several short relationships of his. He'd fuck her every few weeks or so whenever he was in town or she was nearby. He remembered telling this one girl he fucked for a little while about Susie. This was right after this girl told him she thought she was falling for him, her eyes teary, wearing a sincere and almost pathetic smile. For some strange reason, he got pleasure from this: hurting her in her most vulnerable moment, leaving her violated and victimized. In that moment, he was more turned on by hurting her than from fucking her.

He remembered fucking his dormmate's girlfriend who was in town visiting while his dormmate was passed out from drinking too much. He thought maybe the girl was passed out drunk, too, because she didn't move much when he pushed his dick in her tight ass. He remembered having his way with her, ramming at her with everything he had, cumming inside of her ass, then shoving her off the bed and then having to clean up vomit from where her mouth rested on the mattress. That irritated him, so he pulled some phlegm from his throat and spat on her.

He recalled that one time he and a couple of his buddies jumped this gay guy at a bar for no reason at all except for the fact that he was queer, and it'd be fun. He remembered bashing the back of his head in with repeated strikes as the faggot lay there facedown, unconscious. His two buddies tried to pull him off and he didn't talk to either of them after that, the pussies, trying to protect some cocksucker.

He remembered coming home from college for break and doing a bunch of coke he had scored off a trade from these car stereos he had broken out of his schoolmates' cars. At home, he found some cash and jewelry—gold and silver and what looked like a wedding band—in his mother's drawers and, as he liked to call it, "borrowed it," to get some more coke. He didn't find anything else throughout the entire house after spending well over an hour rummaging through everything, every drawer, under every mattress. This pissed him off. He couldn't get coke but scored some meth and then walked by Susie's. After seeing her car was there but her husband's was not, he decided to knock. She opened the door and pulled him inside, where they snorted the meth and then fucked raw until neither of them could breathe.

He remembered hearing what he thought was a car pulling into the driveway with squeaky brakes, but ignored it and continued his ramming of Susie from behind. They were dripping sweat, and it stank like dirty sex, which he could almost smell again in that moment. He remembered thrusting and thrusting and her moaning and moaning and the way her fat ass felt bouncing off his abdomen and how her juices glistened on his skin. He remembered seeing Mr. Toungate's stunned eyes from around the doorway. He threw Susie off of him. Mr. Toungate ran toward the shotgun leaning up against the corner. As fast as a second was—it seemed like slow-motion—he heard the sound of a gun cock and a woman's scream like he had never heard, an indescribable sound, a terrified ear-piercing squeal. There was a deafening blast and a bright flash of light and then Susie's limp body slung up against the wall with half her head and brains splattered above her. And then, there were the shaken eyes of Mr. Toungate again.

He wanted to cry for Susie, seeing her brains exploded into chunky pieces of orange and red, but no tears came. He wanted to plead with Ryan's dad, Mr. Toungate, but no words came. Then were the black holes in the end of the barrels facing him, the cock of the gun, Mr. Toungate's crazed light blue eyes, the piercing blast, and the flash of blinding white...

He continued on this walk for hours—*or could it be longer?*—turning back now and again only to see the exact image behind him that he was entering into: an infinite path coming and going. No matter which way he turned, he was completely entrapped by an unbounded cornfield. And Goddamn it, he hated cornfields. Ice shot through his veins as he turned back from a sound he thought he heard, but there was nothing.

The pain in the bottom of his feet from the rocks was growing. The bottoms were raw, his arches bruised, the outer layer of tenderized skin beginning to peel. The soft breeze blew and felt nice on the back of his ears and neck, but not as nice as it had earlier. He didn't know how much farther he could walk, how much energy he could muster, but he felt he had no choice but to continue. This never-ending path coming and going and the infinite cornfields spanned far beyond what his eyes could see. Many hours passed and after what seemed like even days had passed—*or could it be longer?*—he simply quit counting.

There was no end in sight, nor was there a beginning.

THE BOX

THEN

"Booo," grumbled an obnoxious drunk who sat a couple tables from the stage, red-faced and swollen, a fraternity boy turned middle-aged asshole.

"Ah, here we go," Ron said of his first official heckler now that he had become a legitimate headlining comic at a sold-out show. He had battled hecklers before. He'd seen this same dickwad or an equally stupid version hundreds of times, having worked his way up through the local venues that could barely afford to keep their lights on and smelled of damp, rotting wood and ancient cigarette smoke, but this was different. This was the big leagues. His lips curled upward at the ends as his heart beat with an anticipatory excitement. "We got a live one, folks."

"You're a clown," the heckler said louder than he needed to, his words marinated in booze.

"Yeah?" Ron said, pacing the stage for a moment, looking down and huffing into the mic. "How much did you spend on these, uh—" he did air quotes with his free hand, "*clown* tickets, for you and your a...lady?"

"Too much," the dickwad said, snorting, looking over at his date, smirking proudly from his clever comeback.

Ron continued pacing the stage but more slowly, more confidently, his brain firing over many potential comebacks in his unlimited arsenal. He eyed the man. "Well, we can agree on that, by the looks of that tie you found on the clearance rack of Kohl's and that shitty fucking haircut. And what is that thing on your head, anyway? A fucking coyote?"

Laughter.

Ron looked off in thought. "Hey, stylist, I'm going for a—" he pretended to fluff his hair, "a rabid coyote look. You got anything like that?"

More laughter.

"You suck," the dickwad said loudly, desperately trying to stay afloat but knowing the ship was going down. His eyes were wild and bouncing around, the captain of the titanic running up on a fucking Ron-shaped iceberg.

"Look, buddy, we both know you ain't on no clown budget. You shoulda just took the lady to the backseat. Let me give you a little tip, something I learned long ago: there's no need to spend money on impressing a hooker."

There were some gasps with a few laughs sprinkled throughout the crowd.

"Oh, hey, come on," Ron said. He stood still at the very front of the stage, smirked, and eyed the heckler's date. "Well, *are* you impressed?"

"Fuck you!" the heckler said as he and his date got up.

The audience oohed as if they were watching some disgusting rats get exploited by Jerry Springer.

The guy stared at Ron with both hate and fear in his eyes, his ship now at the bottom of the Atlantic. Trying to save face, he said, "How bout I wait for you outside?"

"Why don't you meet me on the playground?"

The jerk's head about exploded before his unlucky date grabbed his arm and they stomped out, the rest of the crowd applauding their exit.

"Make him wear a condom, please," Ron said, shaking his head. "For fuck sake."

NOW

Ron stared ahead at the endless line of brake lights. He would've sighed but there were no sighs to give.

Fucking traffic.

It was the peak of summer, the eleventh straight day above one hundred degrees, and hot air blew from his vents. Ron's polka-dotted arm hung out the window, his mouth open and panting like a dog that just fetched way too many balls, the sweat and white makeup stinging his eyes like hundreds of tiny pissed-off scorpions, the walls of his suffocating Hyundai Accent-turned-sweat lodge closing in around him. He had put off spending the seven hundred fucking dollars on the new fucking compressor, *and why the fuck can't I get a break?*

Ron gripped the wheel with his right hand so tight his knuckles hurt as he snorted pure frustration, grinding his teeth.

A young family in a shiny new SUV pulled up in the lane next to him. He looked over briefly, seeing the entire family—Mom, Dad, Jill, and little Johnny staring over with wide eyes and cartoonish grins—before turning away. Ron let out an exhausted sigh and closed his eyes. *Come on, Ron. You're a clown, for fuck sakes.* He looked back over, honked his red nose with his fingers, and waved. The family waved back, their happy little eyes lit up with joy. One thing was for certain: his life was a miserable piece of shit with little joy to be found for himself, but at least he brought joy to others, and that's what comedy was all about.

The stop-and-go traffic continued as the SUV full of satisfied customers pulled ahead with a story to tell all their friends over the next few days about the funny clown stuck in traffic. Behind them came a young hotshot in a brand-new yellow Corvette convertible. Somehow this guy—or a clone of this guy—always seemed to show up at the most *opportune* moment, as if there were some asshole-producing factory making these dickwads that had only one function: give Ron shit. The aging Ken doll with artificially taut skin and a tan five shades too dark looked over and chuckled before bursting into full-on obnoxious laughter. Ron honked his red nose and waved, always the showman. He could see this asshole mouth the words "What a fucking asshole" to whomever was on the other end of the Bluetooth.

More laughter.

Joy.

Ron pulled up to the party and parked along the curb. He walked up to the house, the ear-piercing ruckus of children's screams just a door away. He stood there, playing out the next hour of his life, tempted to turn around and get the fuck as far away from there—from everywhere—as he could, but he knew there was no turning back; no place to go. There was no escape from the hell he was living. To say he needed the money felt like a drastic understatement, and he was already fifteen minutes late. *Fuck me.* He rang the doorbell, hearing the ruckus quiet some.

A blonde woman in her early thirties that could've been a model before kids sucked the vibrancy and try-to from her opened the door. She eyed Ron with a look of disappointment or disgust or maybe both, turned and said, "Well, our clown is finally here." She turned back, glanced at her watch, and shook her head. "Well, come in," she said, straight-faced. "I'll gather the kids."

"I'm sorry. Traffic was horrendous," Ron said as the woman turned from him mid-sentence. He carried the plastic tote of party props inside, watching the curvy woman's round soft ass walk away. *I'd wear that ass as a fucking mask,* he thought, visualizing her bent over and his face deep between her cheeks, lapping up her salty pussy juices while his nose fucked her dirty asshole.

An older woman's sharp eyes met his from the other room, goring his sexual fantasy. Ron, caught by the old maid, reflexively smiled. The wrinkled bag of skin rolled her eyes and turned away, repulsed.

The adults corralled the ten or so kids into the living room to watch the *Amazing Ron* do his act. No longer consisting of vulgarity, crudeness, and spending the majority of his time talking about drinking booze, snorting drugs, and eating peanuts from random recently-divorced women's assholes while they howled like rabid hyenas, his new schtick was fondling and shaping balloon animals. Long gone were the mature audiences trying to fill an Andrew Dyce Clay void in their hearts. Ron's new audiences sat criss-cross applesauce, some probably still sucking their mother's tit while old grannies watched with fire in their eyes and hate in their hearts. He told himself at the beginning of every kid's party: *it's just an hour.*

One hour of absolute death.

He willed himself through the mind-numbing hell and with a couple fart jokes, some intentionally-failed magic tricks for laughs—*oh there isn't a rabbit under this magic hat after all...I guess it ain't so magic...I'm such a loser, yadda fucking yadda*—and close to a dozen sculpted balloon animals, one for each child at the party; there was laughter and applause, and his job was done, having only a lost a little more of his tortured, worthless soul.

Ron collected his things as the kids instantly forgot about the clown and went on to the next thing.

"Yes. YES, that's it," some guy said. "It *is* him."

Ron sighed, knowing exactly who *he* was and where this conversation was headed. It was just a part of being the *Amazing Ron.*

The guy walked over. "I've seen you." He pointed and wagged his finger at Ron, a big satisfactory smile on his face.

"Well," Ron said, snapping the lid on the tote holding all the party gear while avoiding eye contact with the dipshit, "I'm not the only clown in Funville."

"No, like—" the guy paused, the memory becoming clearer by the second. "We've seen you in Vegas...at the Dragon Room." He turned toward the gaggle of MILFs and the disgusted old bird with the incriminating eyes. "Right, honey?" The blonde with the round ass smiled. The man turned back to Ron, his excited grin subsiding as his mind went somewhere far away for the moment.

"No," Ron said, shaking his head, wanting to stop this train in its tracks. "Not me."

The guy kept on, a concerned look on his face. "How did you...I mean—" He caught himself and did his best to change from the awkward path he was headed. "I guess birthday parties are a pretty good gig. Less hecklers, am I right?" He forced a laugh through tense jaws. "Man," he said, staring at Ron while shaking his head in utter disbelief that such a bigtime headlining comedian would stoop as low as doing children's birthday parties. "You were so funny. I can't believe you are in our house right now."

Ron knew the man was unaware how these conversations dug into his intestines like daggers and ripped at his soul.

"Alright, buddy," Ron said as he picked up the tote of party props. "Back to the looney bin I go."

Ron felt it best to not engage the folks who recognized him from his past successful life, avoid them at all costs. They were like an unwitting plague come back from when he wasn't some fucking loser clown piece of shit to mock him. Natural comedians had a knack for bringing joy to others, but also the uncanny ability of inflicting pain on themselves. Ron was no exception. These moments always sent him back into that dangerous territory of regret and self-destruct mode.

Ron left the party and stopped off at Happy Time Liquors on the way home. He sat the plastic fourteen-dollar bottle of whiskey on the counter to be rung out.

"Oh," the young cashier who was probably voted most likely to be a failed musician by his high school classmates said with a pouty face. "Why so glum?" He laughed. *The whole sad clown irony thing.*

Ron paid him, and with the scowl that's been with him since the recent fan encounter, honked his nose. He threw up a quick animated smile, eyes big, white teeth on full display, before his face reverted.

The cashier laughed, grinning ear to ear, and said aloud to himself as the clown left with his bottle of cheap liquor, "I fucking love clowns."

***

Ron pulled into his apartment complex and parked his car-turned-sauna, rolled up the windows, and wiped the sweat from his face and eyes, smearing the greasy white face paint on his hands. "Yeah, honey. I'm still here." He held the sweat-drenched phone to his ear with his shoulder as he locked the car, hugging the whiskey bottle to his chest, and walked to the stairway that led to his apartment. His daughter Lillian from a really bad mistake thirty years ago was on the other end. "What? No, I'm fine. It's just—" He was short of breath from the hot car, and the stairs didn't help. Ron had never been in shape, or really taken care of himself at all, for that matter. He had a whole bit about gyms being nothing but homo cesspools and squawked at the idea of "working out," but damned if these fucking steps didn't become more treacherous by the day. *Maybe the gays were onto something.*

"Dad?"

"Yeah, honey," Ron said, struggling to breathe, almost to the top of Mount Everest. "I'm here."

"You sound like you're dying. You sure you're okay?"

Despite Lillian's mother being a fame-chasing whore and her dad being an alcoholic clown, she'd somehow turned out alright, normal, maybe even decent, which blew away any expectations Ron had for his and that cantankerous bitch's spawn.

"The damned AC went out," Ron said. "I know, honey. I know." He stopped at the top of the stairs, noticing a black box sitting at his doorstep. "I a—" *What the fuck is this?* "I need to call you back. There's a package," he bent down and picked up the box, "or *something.*"

The black box was a little smaller than a shoebox and made of solid wood, making it much heavier than it looked. He turned it this way and that way, looking it over. The surface was smooth and had no labels or shipping info. "Okay. Love you, too. Tell the boys Grandpa Ron loves 'em." He moved his gaze from the box to the phone, irritated at his daughter's incoming response. "Okay, OKAY, already. How 'bout you bring them out to see me, huh? This works both ways, you know." He closed his eyes and breathed through his nose, lowering his tone before saying, "You know I don't like flying." Lillian said something to make him snort a small laugh. "Okay, deal. Bye, honey." He pressed End, unlocked his front door, and carried the mysterious box inside.

Ron's apartment was pretty basic: a couch and recliner that didn't match, a tv mounted on the wall, no pictures other than the ones of his daughter and two grandsons he had only seen a handful of times stuck on the refrigerator, each picture aging them by a year or so and him by ten.

He set the black wooden box on the table and just stared at it for a moment. He picked it back up. "What are you?" He felt around on its smooth exterior before finally realizing where the edges were to open it. He gripped it and pulled, but nothing. He tried harder to no avail, bending one of his fingernails back. "Ah. Mother fucker." He decided to grab a butter knife from the kitchen drawer. He delicately slid the knife end into the small seam and pried it wider and wider until the box came open. Ron gasped and his eyes doubled in size as he dropped the box like scorching hot coals and stumbled back, falling to the ground, his side and elbow taking the brunt of the fall. "Ow!" He lay on the floor, grabbing his side and rubbing his arm, looking up at the box now fallen open on the table, its unworldly insides exposed. His heart pounded up against his sternum like an angry gorilla trying to break free of its cage as he tried to catch his breath and regroup. "What the fuck?" He worked to pull himself up from the ground and slowly—very slowly—inched toward the box and that hideous...*thing*, never taking his wide eyes from it.

Bang. Bang. Bang.

The knock at the door startled Ron, making him belt out an unfamiliar, high-pitched shriek.

"Is everything okay in there?" said the raspy woman who lived below him, always the first to stick her nose into everyone's business and who treated the complex grounds like her own personal ashtray.

"Fuck," Ron let out under his breath. *Why now?* "Yes," he said loud enough for her to hear from outside. "I'm fine."

"Are you sure? I heard a loud—"

"Yes, Julie. I'm sure," Ron said through gritted teeth, wishing the nosy neighbor would just disappear. How she hadn't died from lung cancer made him question if lung cancer, or God for that matter, even existed. She was a fucking chimney, if chimneys were haggard old bitches who went out of their way to ruin everyone's days she could within the proximity of this entire complex, centering her focus around this particular building.

He quietly waited and listened for Julie to leave, hoping she *wouldn't* tumble down those steps and choke on the tar and menthol that had filled her lungs up over the years. After a few seconds of rasp-free silence, he focused his attention back on the box. He took in as deep a breath as he could to compose himself, counted to three, then four, then five, before reluctantly but speedily lunging toward the table, grabbing both halves of the mysterious black box and shutting away the horrible thing that was inside. He jumped back, his eyes stretched wide, his empty hands held up with palms out, showing the box he was unarmed, an instinctive move from his *few* run-ins with the law.

When nothing happened, he lowered his hands and relaxed his posture. He walked way around the table and that goddamned thing, whatever it was, grabbed the bottle of cheap whiskey, twisted off the top and took a swig. He had become accustomed to bottom-shelf whiskey as of late, so his throat had built up a tolerance to the venom. He smacked his lips a couple times and wiped the burning remnants from his mouth, never taking his eyes from the box. He leaned up against the counter, bottle in hand, wondering what the fuck he had just brought into his home. *Where did it come from? Who put that...thing inside of it? What the fuck is that* thing *anyway?* He took another swig that warmed his entire chest and wondered what he was supposed to do with it. He couldn't keep it here, but...

His mind went blank for a moment. Ron had seen a lot over his lifetime of debauchery, but his brain had no experience handling something like *this*, whatever *this* was. He had to think on it. For now, the best short-term idea he could come up with until something better came along was to cover it with a dirty tee shirt, which he did.

Out of sight, out of mind.

***

Ron woke to his heart racing, maybe from a nightmare that was already lost forever in an endless stream of forgotten dreams, or maybe it was just his heart telling him to fuck off with the liquor-infused, worthless blood it had to pump. He looked toward the alarm clock, trying to focus through the drunken haze. There was one blurry clock, then two, then one again before his eyes finally adjusted enough to read the red eleven thirty-two on the display. *Fuck.* Next to the clock was the bottle of cheap whiskey he had all but killed. There was enough light brown liquid at the bottom for one or two more swigs, tops, probably made up mostly of his own backwash. He lay back onto the bed and looked at the ceiling, his head throbbing with slow, intense jolts of pain. As he lay there, he heard a lot more voices outside than normal, then rhythmic heavy steps up the stairs and a firm *knock-knock-knock* on his door.

Ron sighed and pulled himself up from the bed, his body stiff and sore, every movement sending more waves of pain crashing through his skull. He swallowed the rotten taste and then got a whiff of himself. He felt and smelled like a punching bag a bunch of hobos pissed on after beating the shit out of. He laughed, but even that hurt.

Bang. Bang. Bang.

"I'm coming. I'm coming," Ron said, the banging at the door reverberating inside his skull, the echoes growing louder rather than quieting.

He opened the door, his eyes not ready for the blast of daylight. There was an officer there.

"Hi," the officer said, caught a little off guard. He stared skeptically at the drunk guy with half his face smeared in white makeup and his barely opened eyes framed by swollen, dark bags, before peering around him into the dark apartment. "Sorry to disturb you. I'm Sergeant Calloway."

The king of mustaches.

"We're doing a wellness check on your downstairs neighbor. Just wanted to see if you had seen her or know where she might be?"

"Who?" Ron reflexively let out, his sluggish brain not yet prepared for questions. The morning sun felt like fucking daggers in his eyes. "Julie?" He looked down, seeing a few other officers and a couple familiar tenants and a goddamned cigarette butt at the top of the steps. *I swear that woman leaves a fucking trail wherever she goes.*

"Yes," the officer said. "She didn't show up to her job this morning."

"That old bat had a job?" Ron said, and then thinking out loud, mumbled, "Other than terrorizing her neighbors?"

The officer just stared flatly and said, "No one has been able to get ahold of her. The landlord went inside her apartment, and she isn't there, but all her belongings are there: her phone, her purse."

Ron thought about the black box and then how he wished—only briefly—that that nosy bitch would...disappear. His stomach turned, and not from the whiskey as the unfamiliar feeling of guilt hit him in the balls.

"Were her a...cigarettes in her purse? Cuz she don't go nowhere without those fucking things." Ron chuckled nervously.

"I'm not sure," said the officer. "Anyway—" he eyed Ron, then glanced around him into the apartment, "if you see her or think of any place she might be, let us know."

"Sure," Ron said and just stood there in the doorway, watching the officer walk down the steps but only seeing bits and pieces from yesterday: the box, the grotesque fucking thing inside the box, Julie.

He *had* wished her to disappear, *but no,* he thought. *No fucking way. This ain't no goddamned genie bullshit.* He shut the door and stared over at the box covered by the dirty white tee shirt. "Nope," he told himself, unconvincingly at best, before getting frustrated for allowing such a ludicrous idea to fester. "Alright," he said, working himself up like a boxer before a fight. He marched over to the table, removed the shirt and picked up the black box, holding it out as far from his face as he could, examining it. His eyes burned. He set it down and picked up the butter knife. He shook his head and said to himself, "Here we go." He pried open the box and quickly tossed it back down, stepping back and doing his best not to look inside. The thing he had seen last night or thought he'd seen didn't reveal itself, but there was a strange shift in energy. The curly hair on his arms danced as if there was electricity in the air. He caught his breath for a moment and thought of how he could test his crazy theory, hopefully putting the stupid fucking idea to rest for good. His mind drew a blank until he saw the almost-empty bottle of cheap whiskey from yesterday, sitting on his nightstand.

He swallowed and made his wish. The bottle instantaneously filled. He fell back against the wall, his eyes lost in the bottle that was magically full again, his mind lost in La-La Land.

A magic fucking lamp box? he thought. *You gotta be kidding me.*

He peeped through the blinds at the police and other folks dispersing below, paranoid of getting caught for something. *I haven't done anything wrong, right?* he asked himself. *Surely old Julie would show up,* he assured himself. Surely he didn't wish her away into oblivion.

He stood there at a loss, staring at the bottle of whiskey freshly replenished as if he hadn't even opened it. *That old bitch is gone.* He chuckled at the insanity and quickly moved onto bigger things than obliterating his neighbor who nobody liked anyway, the woman always in everybody's business, an annoying scourge on the earth if there ever was one. If the box were granting him wishes, and he wasn't going fucking insane—or at least, more insane than normal—he couldn't wait to try his luck again with this thing, and what better object to wish upon than that piece of shit AC compressor that has made his life a living hell this summer?

***

Ron clowned up (that's "got ready" in clown talk): got into his polka-dotted clown suit and oversized red clown shoes, painted his face in white and his lips an exaggerated red. He was ready for the little gig down at the tech office, a birthday clown-a-gram for one of the employees. A quick one hundred and fifty bucks for a few giggles. And hell, maybe he'd get to see some hot women in short office skirts. He always loved broads when they put on that *business professional* act, pretending to be important contributors when everyone knew the only reason they got the job was because their male bosses wanted to fuck 'em.

He got in the car and cranked it up, then said aloud as the hot outside air flowed from the vents, "I wish the AC blew cold air again."

Just like that, the hot outside air traveling through the car passed through the now-working compressor and chilled to an icy sixty degrees before leaving the vents. The cold air hit Ron and a smile the size of Manhattan grew across his face. "Ha. HaHA!" He laughed hysterically, fanning the cold air into his mouth like he was ingesting the fountain of youth—savoring the moment for several minutes—before getting on his way.

***

Ron pulled up to a stop light and noticed a fat kid with red hair in a horizontally striped shirt standing on the sidewalk eating from an ice cream cone and wondered, *why the stripes? The kid's already got enough problems. Why put him in fucking stripes? And the ice cream... What's wrong with his parents? Are they trying to get him killed at school?*

The hefty boy looked over, saw Ron, and laughed. He waved, and Ron waved back. Then the kid gave the bird to Ron and slowly and deliberately mouthed "You suck," before licking his ice cream like a spoiled pig, the cream melting and running down his chubby little fingers.

"Oh, I suck?" Ron said aloud. *Everyone's a fucking heckler.* "Why don't you go ahead and do the world a favor now and get hit by a truck, you little sh—"

Ron's words were stopped short by a loud boom and a cloud of bright red mist that stuck to the air as the truck's front bumper and radiator met the large boy, catapulting him roughly sixty feet from the impact.

The truck had come flying out of nowhere and hopped the curb, smashing only into the boy as if targeted before stopping. The traffic light turned green, but no one moved. Everything was completely still for a second or two as if time itself had stopped, before snapping back into the current frenzied moment. One woman fainted while others—including the driver of the truck—followed the trail of ropy innards stemming from the front of the truck, racing over to the boy whose limbs were those of a tangled puppet, lying motionless, framed by an expanding puddle of blood. The pointy end of the waffle cone protruded from his eye, the old-fashioned vanilla and sprinkles now a part of his brain. Various pitches of screams came from every direction.

THEN

"You suck!" some guy from the audience called out.

"Oh, jeez," Ron said, putting his head down, sucking on the back of his teeth, and slowly walking the stage. "There's always one, folks."

"You're not funny!"

"Yeah, well—" Ron huffed into the mic and paced the stage for a moment while he went through the list of comebacks he'd retained over the years of battling bottom-shelf scumbag hecklers like this one. "The only thing in here that gets more laughs than me is your sorry excuse for a cock." He looked to the guy's date. "Sorry, ma'am. You probably aren't aware, but you're in for a second comedic act later tonight when this douche drops his pants."

The heckler stood up and mouthed something, his voice drowned out by the crowd's laughter.

"Who would've thought someday I'd be opening up for this guy's tiny cock?"

More laughter from the audience.

"My middle school aptitude test said nothing about this," Ron said, looking down in thought. "I don't know."

The heckler, quickly losing ground, mouthed some other unintelligible shit, unable to out-compete the crowd's laughs, and began unfastening his belt.

"Whoa, pal," Ron said, shaking his head No. "Don't cut into my act. You can embarrass yourself later."

Before the drunk, flustered heckler could get his dick out, security was there to firmly escort him and his date to the exit, the woman's head buried in shame, obviously regretting whatever decisions led her to this point: being kicked out of a comedy show because the dipshit she let fuck her was about to pull his dick out in public. The audience cheered and applauded the two burly security guards ridding them of the problem. Before leaving the room, the heckler threw Ron a double bird and mouthed some other stupid shit, most likely an empty threat of some sort, the veins in his forehead and neck bulging, his face crimson with anger.

"Eh," Ron said in his best Tony Soprano voice. "Get outta here."

NOW

Ron informed the contact at the office party that he was running a little late due to an accident that left the traffic all kinds of fucked. He didn't mention wishing the kid to his death, or how a boy's blood and goopy intestines look a lot different outside of the body than in. But he hadn't *wished* it, had he? He just sort of...thought it.

Ron pulled off at the first bar he came across. He ordered and took two shots of whiskey, too shaken to pay any mind to the few spectators already drowning their sorrows before half the day had passed. He couldn't shake the image of that chubby little boy's freckled bratty face, chowing down on his ice cream cone, completely unaware that his life was about to come to an abrupt end. *That poor kid. What about his parents?* Ron thought about his daughter Lillian when she was that age, trying to recall times spent with her, but they were few and hazy, Ron always on the road or inside a random woman—any woman who let him—never home, never really a father. *Am I a killer? I didn't mean to, right?* Ron fought back the guilt and wiped away the single tear before it broke free. He paid his tab and left the dingy bar, hoping the booze would hit his bloodstream and calm him down some by the time he got to the party. He didn't know what to think right now; he just needed to get through.

*****

The office of the party looked to have been designed by a millennial with an unlimited IKEA store card—boxy furniture, modern, simple, comfort and functionality the last things on the designers' minds. Young professionals walked around smiling, feeling way more important than they actually were, Mom and Dad's money making them bachelors of social arts, marketing, business, some other degree that all their friends had.

Ron was led past the labyrinth of cubicles to the conference room by a blonde receptionist with the bluest eyes he'd ever seen and fantastic tits. *Nothing like a pair like that to get your mind off of murdering a kid.* She had some writing—*maybe Arabic?*—tattooed on the inside of her forearm, which Ron thought was an odd statement. She was as American homegrown as one could be, despite fighting it with tattoos and Elsa-white hair and dark lipstick and staying as far away from the sun as possible.

"We'll bring them back in fifteen," the receptionist said, and smiled cutely. "Penelope is going to *love* this."

Ron just looked at her, dreamt of those fantastic tits slapping his face. And without even a second to consider even the slightest possibility of potential consequences, his brain fired, and the wish was made.

Penelope did in fact love Ron's little birthday-gram, as did the tech nerds and young professionals who seemed just way too happy to be human. *What planet do these people come from?* Ron wondered.

Ron packed up his bag and walked to his car, discreetly followed to the parking garage by the big-titted blonde who apparently had a sudden, uncontrollable urge to fuck a clown, which boy did she ever. Ron wondered if his POS Hyundai's suspension could handle the bouncing as she rode him like a rodeo performer, his face all but battered from the slapping of her beautiful tits that were now speckled in white clown makeup. She bucked harder and harder until her breathing stopped for a moment, her body quivering. She squealed like something from another world as Ron felt his cock and entire abdomen get wet, her juices running between his legs and onto the seat.

"Fuck," Ron said, thrusting harder.

The squirting just kept coming and coming, drenching Ron and his car seat, running down onto the floorboard, the juice like ice on his skin, before her head fell on Ron's shoulder and she released a deep, exhausted sigh.

"Fuck," she said.

"Yeah," Ron said between breaths with an oversized grin only a clown could make. "Fuck."

"Fuck. No," she said, trying to duck and slide as low as she could.

"What—what is it?"

"It's my fucking boss. Also...my boyfriend."

"Oh fuck," Ron said, before hearing the guy, super happy and so important.

"Hey, clown man!" he said, making his way to Ron's car. "You're the best. Penelope really—" He stopped at the window, looked at Ron, then his girlfriend who was naked and trying to hide atop of Ron, whose clown pants were down, then back at Ron. His face contorted and changed to various shades of red as the anger rose and his fists clenched.

"Laura?" he said through tense jaws. "What the fuck?" Steam shot from his ears and nose as Ron pushed the girl to the driver's side, opened the door, and forcefully shoved the girl out of the car and onto the ground.

"Hey," she yelled, confused and angry, obviously never having been kicked out of a car by the same dirtbag clown she just got caught fucking.

"You son of a bitch," the guy said, trying to pry the car door open.

Ron jammed the key into the ignition and instinctually had that thing in reverse before the key even turned. The tires squealed. Ron saw the disheveled blonde picking herself up from the ground, those beautiful fucking fun-bags hanging out there for the world to see smeared with Ron's white face paint—he could still taste those beauties and feel her pussy juices on his cock and ass, everywhere, the driver's seat flooded. *We got ourselves a squirter, folks!* She had one high-heel in hand and the brightest, most confused blue eyes he had ever seen. Then came the crazy pissed boyfriend charging right at him. Ron shifted to drive and hit the gas, peeling out and away, the guy only landing a couple hard punches to the rear window and fender. Ron watched the guy in the rearview become smaller and smaller before disappearing entirely.

Ron's grip around the steering wheel tightened. He had enough problems without some fucking magic box that grants wishes, makes old hags vanish, kills spoiled brats, and almost gets his dick torn off by angry boyfriends. "Fuck!"

***

Ron pulled up to his apartment and parked. His phone rang. He looked at the caller ID. "You've got to be kidding me." It was his ex, the mother of his daughter. "What does this bitch want now?" He hit Ignore. The phone immediately started ringing again. He checked the display. Yep. It was her with her annoying fucking persistence.

He shook his head and sighed, knowing he had only one option.

"Yeah," he answered.

"What are you doing, Ron?" she said in a tone that only a severely scorned woman could pull off.

"What do you mean, what am I doing?"

"Your daughter, Ron. Your grandkids? Ring a bell?"

The phone was silent for a few seconds.

"Look," Ron said. "Right now is *really* not a good time to—"

"Well, when is a good time, Ron? Because it seems like it is *never* a good time for you."

"Oh, don't you pull this shit right now."

The phone stayed quiet for a moment.

"Just when I thought you couldn't be a bigger deadbeat, you surprise me again."

Ron bit his upper lip, doing his best not to verbally destroy this fucking chronic heckler.

"You know," she said calmly, "maybe it's good that your grandkids don't even know who you are. Probably better that way."

Those words cut deep into Ron, tearing at his abdomen. "Cassandra, stop."

"Stop what? Pointing out what a piece of shit you are?"

"Please, Cassandra. I'm begging you. Stop."

"I fucking...I can't even—" she said, her frustration inhibiting her vocabulary. After a long breath, she said coldly, "I wish I never met you. Fucking loser."

The L word always sent Ron over—there's nothing more painful than the truth—and this time was no different. "Well, I wish I never stuck my dick in that toilet bowl of yours. Sloppy seconds, my ass. Sloppy—" The phone went silent before he could finish his onslaught of crude attacks. He looked at the display and then his call history. The call from Cassandra was gone.

"Oh fuck." He looked off into nothing and his stomach sank to the center of the earth. "Oh fuck, fuck, fuck."

Ron ran up the stairs and, with trembling hands, finally got the key in and unlocked the door. He rushed inside and to the refrigerator, which was a mural of pictures of his daughter and grandsons no longer. The pictures were gone. Ron, frantic, his mouth agape, pulled out and roughly shuffled through each drawer, just hoping that he had forgotten that he had taken the pictures down and put them somewhere, anywhere, but they were nowhere.

Oh, no.

Ron grabbed his phone and scrolled through his contacts, looking for the name of his beautiful daughter who, with one slip of the tongue, he'd just wiped from existence.

"No. NOOOO!" Ron fell back against the counter, his heart imploding, his whole world just torn from him, and then spotted that cursed black box lying open upon the table.

He stood up and stepped toward it. "Bring her back. Bring her back!"

Nothing.

Ron, in the midst of the frenzy, told himself to think. *I have to be more specific.*

"I wish I hadn't picked up the phone and...and I wish my daughter still existed." He sat there, breathing in and out, his chest moving up and down, waiting, hoping.

Still nothing.

No pictures.

There was no Lillian in his phone.

He fell to his knees, now sobbing, the white makeup dripping onto the tan linoleum floor. He looked to the box. "I wish—" Ron had never been so angry or hopeless in all his life. Every muscle tensed, his knuckles and fingers clenched so tightly they throbbed. Through cracked words, he said, "I wish you'd come get me, you son of a bitch."

Ron watched as the slimy little black thing that looked like an overfed, deformed leech slithered out of the box and onto the floor. The creature that seemed to fall somewhere between a hellish slug and disgusting snake inched its way toward Ron, growing rapidly, first outgrowing the box from which it came before coming face to face with the equally-sized clown. Ron's rage-fueled braveness was now replaced with utter fear. Sweat poured down his forehead in white streams. The air was thin as he gasped in and out, his heart *thumping-thumping-thumping.* A portion of the creature's smooth, shiny black skin protruded outward and came within inches of Ron's face, as if it were examining the weak clown of a man. There were no eyes or mouth or anything, just slimy blackness. Ron pulled his head back as far as he could to where it was touching the wall behind him, and turned his face away from the hideous thing. His mouth hung open, and he closed his eyes, short breaths in and out, in and out. It was so close, he could feel the thing's being. Ron steeled himself, and after what seemed like an eternal nightmare, opened his eyes. That's when the creature's mouth—framed by what looked like infinite rows of shark's teeth—expanded wide and lunged toward Ron, swallowing him with one quick chomp. Ron screamed as he swung wildly inside the creature, its walls expanding around Ron's fists like elastic, the jagged teeth tearing into his flesh one twisting row at a time, completely shredding the clown into nothing more than a bloody, well-blended pulp.

The creature slithered its way back toward its home, shrinking down until small enough to fit, and slinked over the box's edge and inside, the clown gone forever, his final wish granted.

The box closed.

THEN

"Oh, boy," Ron said as he stopped mid-punchline. He shook his head and peered over at the guy who wasn't heckling, but worse—being obnoxiously loud and talking over the performance, trying to impress his date. This was a tough crowd as it was, Ron's act just not going over. The last thing he needed was this asshole to throw him off even worse. "Hey, fella."

The guy finally stopped mouthing and looked up at the stage.

"Yeah, big mouth," Ron said. "You. You wanna shut up for a minute so I can go on?"

The guy looked at his date and the others at the table and then spoke up. "Nah." He fanned his hands in front of his face, like wiping away a fart. "You suck."

"Okay," Ron said, now back into normal heckler territory. "I suck?" Having battled assholes just like this one for way too fucking long, the excitement of the fight was gone. He just didn't have it in him anymore.

"Yeah, asshole," the guy piped up. "You fucking suck."

Ron sighed and looked around at nothing, paced the stage for a moment. He wondered if there was an asshole factory somewhere where these guys just fell off the assembly line by the thousands, and at that very moment had an epiphany: he couldn't do this anymore. Standup—because of dickwads just like this one—had become nothing more than a job he had grown to hate.

"You're a fucking—" the guy wrapped his mouth around the next word, "loser."

Ron closed his eyes tightly, biting and sucking on his bottom lip before dropping the mic, jumping from the stage and charging the guy, ending his standup career in a firestorm of swinging fists resulting in a broken nose, busted lip, cracked rib, a massive hospital bill, and an assault charge for the cherry on top. All Ron could hear while getting his ass kicked for those one or two minutes before security got there, was the crowd applauding. At least, he thought...at least he was able to bring joy to some folks, and that's what comedy was all about.

THE END

AUTHOR'S NOTE

If you enjoyed these silly little stories, please review the hell out of them. Reviews and shares on the socials are what sell books for indie authors. Y'all truly are our marketing team, and we appreciate it. Like *really* appreciate it. So thanks, like *really*.

ABOUT THE AUTHOR

Matt Micheli is an award-winning horror and dark fiction writer out of New Braunfels, TX. A recent widower, and a loving dad to a spunky little girl and two husky dogs, he spends his days dabbling in domestication and his nights in tequila or gin, always searching for the next great story.

You can find him on the socials at @MattMicheliAuthor or contact him through www.MattMicheli.com. He loves connecting with readers and folks in the indie writing world.

OTHER WORKS

Scratched
The White
The Vines
Pornageddon
A Halloween Story: The Complete Collection